I0573277

THE TERROR
BEGINS

She was hurrying past the field on her way home when the man stepped out from behind a tree and stood spraddle-legged in her path.

Ginny Lee was uncommonly pretty, a small girl with unusually long legs for someone her size, good legs with finely molded ankles; and her breasts above the rounded hips and very thin waist were large and full, not in a way that gave her a top-heavy look, but a proud, feminine look. Ginny Lee was happy about her looks except for one thing. She needed glasses.

She stood there blinking and squinting, trying to recognize the man who stood there so menacingly.

"Who are you?" she asked, suddenly frightened.

He laughed, took her roughly and threw her down.

3 Day Terror

Vin Packer

PROLOGUE BOOKS

F+W Media, Inc.

Published in electronic format by
PROLOGUE BOOKS
an imprint of F+W Media, Inc.
10151 Carver Road
Blue Ash, Ohio 45242
www.prologuebooks.com

Copyright © 1957 by Fawcett Publications, Inc.
All rights reserved. No part of this publication may be reproduced or transmitted in any form or by any means, electronic or mechanical, including photocopy, recording, or any information storage or retrieval system, without permission in writing from the publisher.

eISBN 10: 1-4405-3698-8
eISBN 13: 978-1-4405-3698-4

POD ISBN 10: 1-4405-5613-X
POD ISBN 13: 978-1-4405-5613-5

This is a work of fiction. Names, characters, corporations, institutions, organizations, events, or locales in this novel are either the product of the author's imagination or, if real, used fictitiously. The resemblance of any character to actual persons (living or dead) is entirely coincidental.

This work has been previously published in print format by:
Gold Medal Books / Fawcett Publications, Inc., Greenwich, CT.

PART ONE

He parked his car in a spoke of the circle surrounding the grassy spot opposite the courthouse. Folks in Bastrop would say that the tall young man with the citified suit and the New York license plates pulled his old Chevy into the Wheel, because even though Bastrop wasn't really a very small Southern town, 1,468 in the last census, with a "city" listing, it was as curious about, and as aware of a stranger in its midst, as any half its size; so it would particularize more in describing him; guess—because of his plates—that he would be one of these Yankees who said his final g's and all his r's; and speculate some as to his business.

But because he arrived at 10:45 on that rainy Friday evening at the beginning of September, when most in Bastrop were at home, still watching the late show down the street at The Alabama, or attending the Eyeball out at the Yellowhammer Country Club, he went unobserved, except for Turner Towers and his wife, who were just pulling out of the Wheel when he yelled at Turner.

"Hey, nigger! Where can I get something to eat?"

Turner told him Porter Drugs over yonder; after, he said to his wife, "Nice mouth he's got—nigger!" then he forgot the stranger; never dreaming there'd be cause to remember him.

But the stranger some weeks back had circled in red on a map, Bastrop, Alabama; had come for a reason; and it wasn't likely that Turner Towers, or anyone else in town, would soon forget him.

1.   *"That's just the way I am—even in
          Paradise I'd know all the wrong people."*

THAT NIGHT Delia Benjamin got back to town; the first face she saw was his face—the stranger's. He held open the door of Porter Drugs for her.

A moment before, driving through the familiar streets of Bastrop with her mother, she had wondered why she had come home. She had wondered that just after she had asked her mother to pull in at Porter Drugs so she could buy cigarettes, and her mother had answered:

"Right off the bat—in buying your cigarettes! Delia, now, *that* won't make a good impression."

Delia knew it was futile to say the hackneyed, that women smoked quite unashamedly nowadays—even those who *weren't* divorced; knew too that her mother realized that much, but clung more comfortably to the archaic, and believed that Delia should adopt those standards, "under the circumstances;" because people were going to judge her all the harder now. Mrs. Benjamin's people were the "girls" of the Birthday Club, the "girls" of the Methodist Muses, and the entire congregation of Second Methodist Church.

Delia had said, "I didn't come back to make a good impression," and it was just at that point that she had wondered why she *had* come back; then vaguely recalled lines of a poem in some long-lost textbook that seemed to answer the question: *Home is where when you have to go there, they have to take you in.*

Mrs. Benjamin, voluminous in magnolia-splotched print silk; voluble—some in Bastrop say old Judge Benjamin was talked dead—had removed one white-gloved hand from the steering wheel momentarily, gathered her black nylon raincoat more securely to her shoulders, patted the wiry new "perm," and continued, "I hope you didn't come home to make a tawdry impression either!" Mrs. Benjamin pronounced it *toe-dree*, and thought of it always as the only antonym "good" had. "Not just when everything is nice and it's Music Emphasis Month. Delia, I wrote you that I've been elected a muse, didn't I? I'm Terpsichore until October fifteenth."

Delia's eyes had scanned Court Street as the car turned off West Tennessee and onto it; saw the same low-lying stores and buildings leading down to Courthouse Square, and the Wheel; and there in the shadows by the Wheel, the gray stone figure of the Confederate infantryman, with Porter Drugs across the way.

She had said, "God, it all looks the same. Now, Mama, *do* pull in so I can get cigarettes."

She had thought, it *is* the same too, and I'm not much different.

Mrs. Benjamin had slowed up, saying, "I'm the muse of choral singing and dancing. Gay Porter is Clio, and she's not very pleased about *that,* because you can imagine how little there is for the history muse to do during Music Emphasis Month . . . I wish you wouldn't say God that way, Delia."

"I'll be right back," Dee had said, getting out of the car.

Mrs. Benjamin had shouted after her, "Don't buy two at once, Delia. I think it looks tawdry to buy two packages of cigarettes at once like some chained-smoker."

"Chain-smoker!" Dee had laughed over her shoulder, "and I am!"

Then she was facing him suddenly—this stranger who was holding open the door of Porter Drugs, and he was speaking to her.

He said, "That's a sick habit, chain-smoking."

He smiled, or at any rate his lips tipped in what must have been a smile, and his dark eyes shined unusually bright. He was tall and lean, with a stiff stance to his figure, in the gray flannel suit, ivy-league cut. He seemed to wait for her response. Dee noticed all this, thinking that he sounded like a Northerner, and she was about to answer him in some casual way, when she saw a second face, the face of someone she did know—Jack Chadwick's, a face she had not seen in six years. He was sitting in a booth in the rear of the drugstore. Cass, his wife, was with him, and her back was to Delia.

If Dee had known that they would be in there, she would never have insisted that her mother stop.

Now it was too late to turn back. She drew a deep breath, and her heart, which had paused, rushed to beat again. It was bound to happen eventually, she thought.

She clutched the expensive alligator bag to her side, worried that her short, loosely waved black hair had come down in the rain, making a mockery of the monk's-cap cut which Kenneth had labored over at Lilly Daché; then compensated for that anxiety by remembering that she had automatically done a careful makeup at the airport over in Baldwin; retouched it en route to Bastrop in the car; and that the white linen collar which she had attached a moment before she stepped off the plane was crisp and clean above the tightly fitted jacket of the beige summer suit.

The stranger said something else, but Dee didn't hear it. Then he walked on to the fountain, and she remained at the cigarette counter. In a moment Jack Chadwick would look up and see her standing there. It was not too unlike, she recalled absurdly, the first time *she* had ever seen *him*, when she had been sitting in the back booth, and Chad had been standing in the exact spot she was, back in 1943.

That was the day in June when the temperature was well up into the nineties, and the humidity was killing, the year Judson Forsythe was in love with her, the beginning of that summer when everyone was singing "As Time Goes By." All the girls were speaking in husky voices like the new movie actress, Lauren Bacall, and all the boys were destined to copy what Judson Forsythe was about to do that afternoon in Porter Drugs, if he could ever get Delia Benjamin to stop talking.

Her hair was long then, down to her shoulders, and she had that habit of winding it around her fingers when she was impatient, which she was; but undaunted, Jud kept insisting she be still long enough to look at what he had to show her, kept tapping his finger on a box wrapped in red tissue, tied with white ribbon, set between them on the table. She was easily the best-looking girl in Tate County, and, her dates agreed, the most talkative, taking after both her parents in that fact, but favoring the judge, in spirit, because Delia Benjamin liked to "talk serious."

"Not now," Jud was imploring her, "not when I got something to give you, Dee."

"But I was smack dab in the middle of asking you to explain something to me," she said, "and you won't."

"Well. why don't you ask your daddy, Dee? I don't know what all this withholding tax stuff is . . . Look, 'member *Casablanca* we saw at the Alabama last week?"

"You don't know what the bill is President Roosevelt signed this very day, Jud Forsythe?"

"Oh, I know, but ye gods and little fishes I bought you a dog-damn *whistle*, Delia Benjamin, just like the one Humphrey Bogart gave to Lauren Bacall! 'Member, in the movie?" He shoved the box across to her. "I had it inscribed, too," he said.

Still frowning, Delia took the whistle out of the box and read: "If you want anything, just whistle. J." She said "It's very nice, Jud. Thank you. But it does seem it's a funny place to present it. Right out in the open in the drugstore."

"I did it because of the air conditioning," Judson answered. "Knew you wouldn't want to take a hike out to the Dip in this heat." He'd been looking at his thumbs; blushing, and when he looked up and said, "Well, do you like it? Do you remember the part in the movie, Dee?" she was looking past him toward the front of Porter's, looking at someone standing up there by the door.

"I've never seen *him* before."

"Him?" Judson had swung around in the booth to see the short, wiry young man with the bright red hair, who was buying a package of cigarettes and clowning with Cassie Beggsom. "He's the new boy. Family just moved here from the state of Missouri. Name's Jack Chadwick, only everyone calls him Chad," Jud said; then added significantly, "He's older—he's more Cassie's age, eighteen or so."

Chad told Dee later that he had noticed her that same afternoon; that he had seen her sitting back there looking bored and beautiful and that he'd thought, She's someone I'm going to get to know better, almost simultaneously with her thinking, He's someone I'm going to fall in love with this very summer. But it took him a long time and plenty of cat-and-mouse before he confided this to her. Dee, of course, thought *she* was the cat, never dreaming he had flung himself headlong and heart-sore across her snares, his soul filled to spilling with her after his encounter with the first snare of the series, before he was sure enough of her to tell her the way he felt.

The first one was set at the Yellowhammer Country Club, three days from that afternoon in Porter's. She attended the Friday night dance with Judson Forsythe, and even though, like any good daughter of a Southern belle, Delia Benjamin knew even better than most how to "follow," and Judson Forsythe enjoyed a reputation as an excellent escort on the ballroom, Jack Chadwick and Cassie Beggsom found themselves perpetually pushed, shoved, and jostled by the pair. Chad could hear Jud protesting, "Dee, what *is* the matter with you tonight? You're not paying attention;" and Cass Beggsom decided, "Dee Benjamin's been drinking. She always was a little too precocious for her own good," smiling up at Chadwick with an air of amused tolerance at Dee's antics. Cass liked Dee then and called her "cute;" and Cass, precocious in her own right, already attended the University of Alabama at age eighteen, in her sophomore year, added matter-of-factly: "Dee'll probably be coming to Alabam in a coupla years. I'm going to have to tell the Pi Phi's to look out for her. She'll make good sorority material. A little wild, though."

Cassandra Beggsom was wrong about one thing, right about the other. Jack Chadwick found it out toward the end of that evening, when he went out behind the Yellowhammer to get his car. Sitting in the front seat, playing the radio, Delia Benjamin smiled up at him as he pushed down the convertible's door handle; said, "It's crazy the way music makes you feel, you know? Even the tackiest old pops that rhyme moon and June—you hear them often enough, they begin to get you. Like this one: *We strolled the lane together, laughed at the rain together,*" she sang in an off-key soprano. Chadwick winced. "Oh, I know I can't carry a tune, but lane and rain and all that tacky mush. Still, I don't mind it."

Chad said, "There are worse." He got in beside her, took a package of cigarettes from the pocket of his white linen jacket, lit one, blowing the smoke out in a cloud that she brushed with her hands.

He said, "I'm sorry," and held his arm over near the window. "Look, Cass is waiting for me on the steps."

"I expect Judson will be keeping her company." She smiled at him. "You know my name?"

"Sure," he said, "Cass mentioned it tonight. Said you'd make good sorority material when you go to Alabam."

The radio announcer was talking about corn plasters. Dee Benjamin reached over and turned it off. "I wouldn't go to Alabam for anything," she said. "I don't believe in going to college in your own state, do you? I don't believe in sororities either." She looked at him frowning. "Do you Chad?"

Chad had told Dee later that it seemed like the craziest thing that had ever happened to him, walking back and finding her in his car, the green net gown she wore spilling over his yellow straw seat covers, showing the bare burnished skin at the dip above the incredibly full bosom, white shoulders and soft-looking long white arms, half covered by the matching net stole, and down at the gown's other end, the glistening, silver spike-heeled slippers. He told Dee later that he had wanted to reach out then and there and touch the long coal-colored hair, bring his face close to it and smell it, feel it rub against his cheeks. But he let on none of this that night; he stayed stoic, seemed nonchalant, smoking his cigarette and answering her, "I'm going to *my* state university when I get out of service. It's got the best school of journalism there is, Missouri has."

"That's different." She traced the edge of the net gown with her finger. "You probably know what you want to be, and are going where you can take the right courses."

"I'm going to be a newspaper man."

"Do you believe in sororities?" she asked. "You know what I heard? I heard that the Chi Omegas down at Alabam make their pledges get into a coffin during initiation; and then close the lid on them. I mean, I think that's just awful to imagine. Tempting death like that. Lord knows, I'm afraid enough of dying, are you, Chad?"

He felt the slight pressure of her hand come on his knee, then go. "I don't much like the idea," he said.

"The idea of dying, or the idea of sororities and fraternities?"

"Neither one."

She said, "I don't either. We're liberals, I guess."

"I guess," he said.

They were quiet for a bit. Behind them at the clubhouse the Alabama Blue Notes were playing a raucous jitterbug tune; there was the noise that crickets make coming from the golf links; and out at the cooks' quarters the Negroes were giggling and shouting in a game of craps. A breeze was beginning, stirring the long-leafed pines in the distance, and the haw trees close.

Jack Chadwick finally repeated, "Cass is waiting for me on the steps."

"Do you feel like kissing me before I get out and go on back?" she asked.

He smiled and turned toward her, but saw she wasn't smiling. He looked at her for a minute. He told Dee later that was the very minute he fell dizzy in love with her, but when he reached for her he did it in some mild calm trance; he pressed his lips down on hers for only an instant, then placed her back against the seat with his hands on her shoulders. He straightened, and started the motor.

"I better *walk* back," she said. She got out of the car, and looked back in through the open window, her arms leaning on the edge. "Chad?"

"Hmmm?"

"Take me to see *For Whom The Bell Tolls?* It's coming to the Alabama Sunday."

"All right, Dee," he said.

She paused. He had been looking straight ahead, his profile turned to her. Then he looked at her directly.

"I guess you think I'm a little wild?" she said.

"Cass mentioned something about it earlier. But I wouldn't know."

"You and Cass must have had a good time tonight talking about me."

"You kept bumping into us," he answered.

"Well, she's right about one thing," Delia Benjamin said. "I am a little wild. But she's wrong about Alabam and these coffin closing sororities. I wouldn't belong to one."

"How old are you, anyway?" Jack Chadwick asked.

"Going on seventeen."

He put the car in gear, looked away from her to the rear-view mirror.

"You're all right," she said. "Plenty of room on both sides . . . Chad?"

"Yeah?"

"You're going to be a great newspaperman some day," she said. "There's something about you that makes me know that."

Chad's insides did flips, the first of hundreds of thousands of flips to come in the space of seven years from that night.

Pulling his blue Dodge out of the lot, going slowly up the circular gravel drive to the steps of the Yellowhammer, Chad thought, I'm going to marry Delia Benjamin. Some six weeks after that moment, there wasn't anyone in Bastrop who didn't think the same thing.

Chad never showed that he had succumbed, in the beginning. He enjoyed the chase, because Dee was doing the chasing, using every wile known to woman, and some known only to Dee. But through it all, he could hardly believe that Delia imagined she would have to do any more than crook her little finger to bring him to his knees. For she was possessed with a breath-catching kind of fabulous beauty, that haunted even strangers who had seen her no oftener than once, and that quivered like a just-thrown dagger in the hearts of those who had become obssessed by her, and ultimately dedicated. Judge Benjamin's family was rooted in the traditional and the respectable, and Delia's blood was the good kind that told well. Even more incredible to Jack's mind was the fact that Dee read the national news in the Bastrop *Citizen,* as well as "Social Notes All Around;" and finding that scanty, read her father's copy of the Birmingham *Post-Herald;* that she thought she might go to law school somewhere up North; that she didn't compare Roosevelt with Christ; and that she knew who D. H. Lawrence was, even quoted him on their second date: *You tell me I am wrong. Who are you, who is anybody to tell me I am wrong? I am not wrong . . . In Syracuse, rock left bare by the viciousness of Greek women. No doubt you have forgotten the pomegranate trees - - -*

Jack Chadwick's family was new in town, and while it was rich by Bastrop standards, it was *nouveau riche.* Chad's father sold furnaces out of Birmingham; their only ancestor to fight in the Civil War was some second cousin of Chad's grandfather; and Chad's mother was bedridden with arthritis, a fact that kept her off church committees and away from bridge teas. When Dee wore heels, Chad was shorter. Because he had not gone to high in Bastrop, his "best friends" were back in Bolivar, Missouri. People said that he was a good-looking boy, but not especially handsome; nice enough, but not particularly outstanding.

Yet when Chad and Dee became a steady couple, no one in Bastrop could imagine either going with anyone else.

They were the most devoted pair in town. Neighbors of the Benjamins' on Clock Hill could tell time by the blue Dodge parked in front of Number Nine. When Chad and "Benny" (his name for her) arrived at a dance at the Yellowhammer, folks sighed and felt the evening was finally in full swing. The two of them strolling down Court Street on their way to Porter Drugs for a soda, were as indigenous to Bastrop as the tolling of the tower chimes at the courthouse. They were as bright and alert as a pair of hounds in a duck blind, always amused and off to somewhere, and always seeming to possess some superior secret unavailable to others, who neither loved as much as they did, laughed as often as they did, nor seemed so certainly satisfied within the cocoon of *their* individual pairs.

Enchanted, inseparable, inevitable; admired, envied and extolled—Jack Chadwick and Dee Benjamin were *the ones*. When Chad went off to war, Dee mooned around listening to "Saturday Night Is The Loneliest Night of The Week" on the phonograph, knitted socks furiously for Bundles for Britain, and only occasionally went to a picture at the Alabama, or a dance at the Yellowhammar with Judson Forsythe, who had long since established a "pals" relationship with her. When Chad returned, Bastrop's principal hero, holder of the Purple Heart, the Distinguished Flying Cross, the Air Medal with four oak culsters, and a personal commendation from General Twining, no one was surprised. Special got more special, as the rich got richer; and by the same token, Jack Chadwick and Dee Benjamin took up where they left off, only more so. Judge Benjamin was credited with possessing a shrewd sort of compassionate wisdom when he agreed to allow his daughter to attend the University of Missouri with Chad, on condition they did not marry until after they graduated.

Triumphantly they returned at the end of four years; Jack with a Phi Beta Kappa key dangling from his gold watch chain; Dee with scholastic honors and a cardboard beauty queen's crown painted silver and bedecked with papier-maché roses. They were both unchanged, seemingly the same enamoured couple Bastrop had always smiled on; matured now, with ambitions to revive the floundering Bastrop *Citizen*, taking to it the knowledge they had acquired in journalism school.

Time had failed to raise new idols in their absence. *The*

ones remained unchallenged. That they would make a success of their business venture; that Second Methodist Church would resound with the Wedding March's booming finale "almost any time now"; and that Dee Benjamin would ultimately give birth to any number of wildly healthy, and impossibly beautiful redheaded babies, seemed the only conceivable ending to this idyl.

What had happened between them? Nobody knew the answer; only the facts. Delia Benjamin had called off the wedding two days after she gave the print order for the invitations. She had gone North, run off with a rich New Yorker named Maurice Granger, who had divorced her after three and a half years. She didn't even come home for the judge's funeral in 1952. Nobody referred to her as Dee any more, certainly not as Benny either. She had broken Jack Chadwick's heart into a million sore pieces. People said her two names now—Delia Benjamin—when they spoke of her. She was a bad taste in their mouths, a nervous memory.

That evening in Porter Drugs so many years later, the memory was revitalized. Those few who saw Jack Chadwick wave at Delia Benjamin, saw her walk back and stand talking at the booth, Chad standing chivalrously beside her in the aisle, while Cass stayed seated, regarding her with a certain placid resignation—those few would ultimately describe the scene to the rest, in widely varying ways; but all would agree on one thing: Delia Benjamin was back in town, and the first person she was seen talking with was Jack Chadwick. It was a situation that bore watching.

When Dee got back in the car, her mother said, "So you did get two packs after all. That's just like you, not to heed anything I say. Well, the North didn't change you in that respect."

Dee watched the rain-riddled streets with a steady profile.

"Who was the young man opened the door for you, Delia? Looked almost like Judson Forsythe."

"I don't know who he was," she answered. "I didn't know him."

"See anyone you did know?"

Dee waited until she had touched the match's flame to her cigarette, drew in and let the smoke out slowly. "Chad was there," she said. "and Cass. I said hi to them for a second."

Mrs. Benjamin turned right at the Wheel and headed up

Clock Hill. After a moment she said, "How did he seem to take it?"

Flo Benjamin was a woman who understood everyone's life but her own, and very probably never actually considered the fact that she had one. When Dee was younger, Poppy Belden, or Jud—and even Chad, like all her other friends, would say: "I wish my mom was like yours. You can tell her anything. She's so interested!" And Dee would think of how difficult it was to confide in her mother, to hold her attention. Until she understood that Mrs. Benjamin simply could not concentrate on anything pertaining to herself or the judge or Dee, because what other families did and thought was twice as fascinating. She saw her husband, her daughter and herself, through *their* eyes.

When Dee married Maury, it was as though Dee had ceased to exist. She was a letter, and an occasional voice on long-distance; but to Mrs. Benjamin she was unreal, because Mrs. Benjamin didn't really know Maury, nor anyone who did know him; and after their marriage, few people in Bastrop talked about Delia to Flo Benjamin's face. So she found it difficult to have any opinion of her daughter, any solid basis on which to think of her, save for random thoughts she could not always focus, dutiful thoughts which required a certain strained concentration and were never prolonged; and reminiscences, which were the easiest of all, for they involved other people: Gay Porter's saying, *"Dee and Jack certainly are smitten, Flo. Do you think it's still innocent?"* Or Poppy Belden saying: *"Dee looked so pretty at the dance the other night, Mrs. Benjamin. Everyone and his brother were after her."* Or Jack himself saying —on *that* day—*"I'm empty without her. I'm a shell, Mrs. Benjamin. And I still don't know why she did it."*

Now Delia was home again, and in Mrs. Benjamin's eyes rose like a Phoenix from the ashes, for *they* had met after all these years. People had seen them meet and people would have something to say about it. Mrs. Benjamin, in turn, would have something definite to think about the prodigal. People would come up to Flo Benjamin and mention Dee again in some way, however subtle. She was back and Bastrop would talk about her *to* Flo's face now.

Dee knew this and should have anticipated the way in which her mother would frame the question. Not "how did you feel?" "*What* did it seem like to you, Delia?" But "How did *he* seem to take it?"

Dee said, "You mean was he surprised? I guess he was. We both were."

"No, I mean, how did he seem?"

"You mean did his face turn red, break out in a sweat? Did his hands shake? Knees tremble? I'm sorry to disappoint you, Mama. He was pleasant, calm, and quite poised." Dee knocked the ashes off her cigarette. "Why shouldn't he be? He's married to Cass, and he loves Cass. It's over between us, been over a long time. Over, Mama, and forgotten."

At that precise moment Senior Porter was in the telephone booth in the back of the drugstore, listening to his wife's reaction to the news.

Gay Porter was saying: "Don't think for a moment Jack Chadwick ever forgot Delia Benjamin, or her him! Those kind of *passion* romances are never over, mark my word. At least we can thank God our Troy never got himself into anything like that, even though Poppy wasn't our choice for him. He still married with his head and heart and not because he was under some kind of spell like they were. I used to tell Flo myself I didn't think it was as innocent as she fooled herself into believing, never was and still isn't. Don't care how many years have passed. Notice that Maury didn't keep her long either; even he must have known he got second-hand goods. No, I'm not saying things I don't know, Senior. I'm just saying there's some reason Delia Benjamin is back in Bastrop, and I'd be curious to know." Mrs. Porter gave a high giggle. "Law, right during Music Emphasis Month too—with Flo elected Terpsichore and all!"

In the rain the Benjamin car stopped at the top of Clock Hill. Dee looked through the window at the big, square, three-story red brick house, surrounded by huge boxwoods. It seemed incredible that she would enter there and not find the judge; seemed incredible that she would be alone in that house with her mother.

Almost as though Flo Benjamin had the same thought, she asked with a certain glum finality to her tone, "Ready?" —though she was really thinking: Jack *must* have felt *something*—opening the door on her side.

"Ready," Dee sighed.

The question she had asked herself earlier that evening was no longer vaguely framed, nor answered with some random lines from some forgotten poem. As she went through the wrought-iron gate and entered the yard, it sat in her mind like a yellow-eyed cat leering out from the dark: Why did I come back? What did I come back to Bastrop for?

Mrs. Benjamin, clutching her raincoat around her large body, skipping puddles on her way to the porch steps behind Dee, said, "Everyone said he never loved Cassandra Beggsom; said at the time he was only marrying her out of pity."

PART TWO

The stranger finished his ham on rye, perched on the stool in Porter Drugs; he spooned his coffee and stared at his reflection in the mirror behind the counter. He straightened his black knit tie, smoothed the lapels of his gray flannel suit. Beside him, a man in a T-shirt and worn jeans, drinking a bromo, watched him. The stranger glanced at the man and smiled, but the man looked away.

The stranger wanted a cup of hot coffee; his had cooled while he had been munching his sandwich and watching the girl who had entered the drugstore with him. She'd been standing at the back booth talking to the red headed fellow and the lady with him, and the stranger had taken her all in, from her white collar down the beige suit to the good-looking legs and the blue-strutting high heels. Class, the stranger had decided; hard-assed, big-titted, soft-skinned, long-legged class. Looked like a stranger herself, but knew folks, obviously.

The stranger couldn't get the hot coffee. The druggist was in the phone booth, and the colored boy was in back.

He said to the man in the T-shirt, "How can I get that nigger's attention? Want some hot coffee."

The man answered, "Deacon Allen got his mind on tail comes the end of the evening. Can't nobody but a black bitch in heat get his attention, tell yah. But Senior be back in a minute. You a stranger?"

"My name is Richard Buddy," the stranger said.

"Hi-dee! Name's Duboe Chandler."

Chandler toyed with the half-gone glass of bromo, studying the stranger. "In town long?"

"For a time," the stranger said.

"Got business hereabouts?"

The stranger nodded. "In a way . . . " He sipped some of his cold coffee, set the cup on the saucer with a decisive gesture, swung on the stool and faced the man. "Hear you're going to desegregate your schools this coming Monday?"

"That's the rumor."
"Hear it's a fact."
"It's a nigger fact," the man said, "and a nigger idea."
"And it's going to stand?" the stranger asked.
"What the hell we gonna do?"
"I can tell you," the stranger said, "if you got the time."
Duboe Chandler said, "Shoot!"

2. *"Sure I believe in right, but I'm a politician.
It's like a fat man with a weak heart on a
diet. He'd like nothing better than a stack of
buckwheats with a stick of butter on top, but
he knows if he has it,· it might kill
him . . . ."*

—*Troy Porter*

THE CEILING of the Yellowhammer Country Club was hung with eyeballs made of motley crepe paper and tiny Christmas-tree lights. They dangled from strings, winking and bobbing above the heads of the dancers, and behind the eight-piece orchestra on the bandstand bedecked with dahlias, a large red and white poster ordered the participants to:

ENJOY THE EYE BALL!
Proceeds are being donated to the Tate
County Association for the Blind.

At a back table laden with empty dessert dishes and overflowing ashtrays, Jud Forsythe was saying, "Put it this way, Arnie. Our Negroes aren't like the Deep South Negroes, and we in Bastrop don't feel the way folks in the Deep South do about them. In some parts of the state, you'd as soon try to jump rope in quicksand as integrate the schools, but here it's different. Folks may not like it, but everybody knows it's a court order."

Poppy Porter took this time to excuse herself from the table, and go back to the bar to phone her mother-in-law. The children were staying at their grandparents' tonight, and the way the evening had been going, Poppy knew she and Troy would be out past midnight; felt she ought to check with Gay, even if for no other reason than the fact she knew Troy's mother would disapprove if she neglected to. As she walked down the long room, small but shapely, the new taffeta gown—colored light blue, like her eyes—hugging her figure, the long soft brown hair touching her shoulders, the bangs bobbing along the forehead of her pretty snub-nosed face, she could feel Troy's admiring eyes follow her and thought, At least someone in the Porter family approves of me. And was glad for the good conviviality she and Troy were enjoying with her own family this evening, and with their closest friend, Jud Forsythe. It was wonderful to have Jud along with them again. Everyone in Bastrop felt he had mourned Francie's death long enough; had felt in the first place that Jud had deserved more in a wife than Francie had proved to be, poor thing.

Poppy's father, along with Troy, watched his daughter's exit with an affectionate expression on his thin, bespectacled face, and then answered Jud. "I hope you're right about it. I don't really expect any trouble on Monday morning, but you just never know."

"That's right," Troy Porter agreed. He was almost always in complete agreement with Arnold Belden. Troy's father-in-law had been Troy's mentor since he was a boy; had been the reason Troy had gone North to Belden's alma mater, Harvard, to study law; the reason he had given up his practice down on West Tennessee to run for the state legislature; and the reason he had given freely of his spare time to help the school board, of which Belden was principal, fight against the desegregation suit. If Troy were actually to sit down and analyze Poppy's father's influence on his career, he would probably have to concede that Belden was also the reason for the celebration tonight—for Troy had announced to everyone at dinner that he was going to run for the state senate.

Belden said, "The kids have taken it well enough, from all I can gather—but there are always a few trouble-makers."

His wife, a little like Poppy, wearing fresh white net with a red rose pinned to her gray, loosely-waved hair, shuddered slightly and said, "Yes. Crabb Suggs and his kind."

Jud smiled at her. "Oh, I know. And Gus Chandler and Duboe. But it's in-season; that's in our favor. There's cotton to be ginned; folks are busy."

"Then there's Chad's editorials," Arnold Belden said.

Jud looked puzzled, running his finger along his clerical collar. There were some in Bastrop who said he put on airs, wearing his collar backwards like a priest, but most of them were Methodists who wished secretly that Reverend Baird, their minister, would wear some garment that would distinguish him more from the man on the street; wished too that the services down at Second Methodist had a trifle more flair to them; but always maintained: "We don't need incense and azaleas and red velvet kneepads to warm up to the Lord, like the Episcopalians. Times you'd think they were having a medieval orgy over there on Linn Avenue, instead of a plain old God-fearing Sunday-morning worship."

"But Chad's all for integration," Jud said. "Chad was for it before you, Arnie, or Troy, or any of us."

"I was never for it," Troy Porter snapped; then, noticing Poppy come back into the room, relaxed his face; thought how lovely and sweet she looked—and vulnerable too, he thought, wincing inwardly at the memory of the hurt she had suffered long ago before their marriage. His tone was milder as he continued. "Hell, over the past five years I been taking time off to help Arnie and the school board fight integration. I fought the suit because I thought it was the right thing to do. That doesn't mean I believe in violating a court order now, but it doesn't mean I'm for integration now either."

Jud Forsythe sighed, put his palm up much the way he did on Sundays for the Benedictus. "All right, I didn't mean to say anyone was *for* integration—"

"Chad *is*, though. That's always been obvious." Troy Porter found it difficult to let his anger subside, or to control his hostile impulses whenever Chad's name came up in conversation. "He doesn't come right out and say so in the *Citizen*. Thank God Cass is less radical and has her say in the paper's policies, but he thinks so!"

Arnold Belden said, "Well, he's coming out with it now. That's what I mean, Jud, about his editorials. I think he'll stir things up."

It was while Belden was speaking that Troy looked up

at Poppy's face, and knew something was wrong. He stood and held her chair out for her, seated her, searching her eyes; whispered, "Kids okay?" She nodded, still frowning; still with that expression that said she wanted to say something. Troy knew that look, knew it could spell trouble or trivia; but to Poppy's mind meant all was not well.

Jud was carrying on the conversation, "Chad's only saying we ought to abide by the court decision, as far as I can see."

"Listen" Belden said, "there are all sorts of ways to say that, if it has to be said in the first place. The law's been passed and people respect the law around here. But that's different from liking it. There's something about Chad's editorials that smacks of rubbing folks noses in it, the way you do a dog's in his mess."

"You all talking about Chad?" Poppy asked.

"The same old subject," Troy reassured her. "Integration. The last subject I want to talk about at this point."

"That's the good politician," Jud grinned.

Mrs. Belden sipped her coffee, set the cup on the saucer gently and said, "I agree, Troy. Let's forget Monday for this evening."

Behind them the Choctaw Ramblers were playing "Sweet Molly Malone," and white-coated waiters were clearing the front tables. Jud leaned back and lit his pipe, and Troy ground out a cigarette in the ashtray. There were several slow seconds when no one at the table said anything, then Poppy spoke up. "I just called Gay to see how the children were. She told me the strangest thing."

Troy looked down at her, and when she saw his regard she forced a quick little laugh. "Oh, its nothing serious." She paused, then slipped into the familiar vernacular of the Southern female, her face flushed, "Law, I'd ah liked to die when I heard it."

"Well, heard what?" Troy asked.

"Delia Benjamin," Poppy said.

"What'd old Dee do now?" her husband asked. He'd always admired Dee Benjamin's spunk; always secretly savored the recollection of Dee's jilting Jack Chadwick.

She didn't *do* anything," Poppy said. "She's back."

Jud Forsythe said, "Back here in Bastrop?"

"Yes. Gay said Senior called her, said she was in the drugstore—just a little while ago."

"Good!" Troy said. "That's what the town needs to lift its dragging spirits. You know something about that girl? When I was elected to the legislature she sent me a wire, by golly. Said something about get in there and fight. She was always a fighter." Troy chuckled, shaking his head, and stretching his long knees out under the table. He was a big man with a husky six-foot frame, built solidly, the sort who seemed to belong in the clothes he was wearing this evening—the white linen dinner jacket and black pants, and well-shined black shoes. He seemed at home in the formal attire most people in Bastrop donned only for special events, and then grudgingly.

"Poor Flo," Pam Belden sighed. "She'll have her hands full."

Arnie Belden made a face at her, "Aw, come on, now, Dee's not wild as all that. What? Just because she married herself a Yankee, and chose to abandon Paradise to go live up in the devil's territory?"

"A Yankee—" Pam Belden smoothed her hair with her hands and said softly—"and a Jew"

"Why we got Jews right here in Bastrop," Arnie said. "Come on, now, Pam."

"I never think of them that way."

"Well, they are *that way*. That doesn't sound like you."

Troy broke in, "To see your face, darling, I thought you were going to announce that Duboe Chandler was going to run against me or something! So Dee's back in Bastrop! Hell, I could use her for a campaign manager."

Poppy looked across the table at Jud Forsythe. He met her glance for a brief instant, then turned his eyes away.

Belden was saying, "Seriously, Troy, I think your chances are pretty good. Of course you've got to watch Dave Polk. He's got a good name in the state, and—"

"But he's a bachelor," Pam Belden said. "I know I'd never vote for a bachelor. People like a family man; people trust a man more if he's got a wife and kids. I know—" but she stopped, aware of how what she had been saying might sound to Jud; she stammered, and finished with: "Law, I don't know anything about politics. I ought to just keep my big mouth shut, hmm?"

"No, I think you're right," Troy said, "people got to identify with the man they're voting for. People got to think to themselves, Why he's just like you and me. And you know full well he can be a bigot, a jellyfish, or a Christ, but if people can just have that first chance to think he's like them, then from there on in they'll frost the cake and serve it up. Even God himself had to produce a son to get some respect down here, and a good politician's got to do a hell of a lot more. He's got to go to church, and he'd better have gone to war. He's got to have a wife, kids, a dog and a low-priced car. He can't get caught sinning, but he better seem capable of it. If he likes a squash game, he better learn golf instead—and in the South, he's better off learning how to hunt coon. No matter where he is, he better know how to talk."

Arnold Belden said, "You don't have any trouble doing that, my boy."

"What worries me—" Troy Porter continued, and Poppy, reaching across to touch Jud Forsythe's sleeve, whispered, "Dance, Jud?"

Troy Porter did know how to talk. He had talked so well that he had talked himself into being the youngest member ever elected to the Alabama State Legislature, and in Bastrop—he had talked himself into the hearts of nearly ninety per cent of its citizens. Like people anywhere, hero-hungry and celebrity-beholden, they had hastened to embroider and embellish. Troy became their dream of wish fulfillment, their ego, and in some cases, their id; and he became a kind of living advertisement for their frustrated potentials. They said of him that he was a born winner; won at everything—had, ever since a kid; that he was more handsome than anyone in Hollywood, on TV, or in the picture magazines, and more down-to-earth than Will Rogers, Norman Vincent Peale, or Steve Allen. They said he knew enough to be on the $64,000 Question, and those who weren't already writing Ralph Edwards to say he ought to be on This Is Your Life, wrote the $64,000 Question. Children bragged they played with his children; teen-agers that they "sat" with his children. The males estimated that Troy could screw five times a night, seven nights a week; and the females spoke of his gentle manner, his cowlick, and his soft-laughing dimples, that they'd like to poke, just once, with their finger; just a little, playful poke. Law, what yah think he'd *do!*

He was Bastrop's prodigy and Bastrop's private property, on loan, only, to the government of Alabama. They forgot the wildly undignified episodes between Troy and Poppy before their marriage, just as they forgot lesser embarrassments and all his flaws; and like people awakening sweetly to some remembered dream which had momentarily anesthetized reality, they remembered the dream *they* had manufactured, in the person of Troy Porter.

Jud Forsythe never had to recall Troy's and Poppy's tempestuous times in the years immediately following Dee Benjamin's departure. He had watched from the beginning the gradual recurrent appearance of Jack Chadwick's convertible in front of the Beldens', attempted aimlessly to avoid answering Troy's pained questions: Where's Poppy, Jud? You live across from her, did you see her? Has Poppy talked about it to you, Jud. Look, I've got to know Jud. Can't you level with me? Does she mention it at all? He had seen Poppy slim down to sliver-size when the convertible vacillated between the Beldens' and the Beggsoms', seen Poppy stagger through a myriad gay parties with Chad, as drunk and disheartened as he was, as though she too was cracked-heart-haunted by the ghost of Delia Benjamin, grief-ridden and stunned—only to end those evenings off in a corner alone, crying in a lace hanky, while Chad stood swaying across the room, hanging onto a table in a desperate attempt to steady himself before the sober and sympathetic figure of Cass Beggsom.

Jud—and all of Bastrop—had witnessed the sudden, whip-quick slapping which Troy had administered to Poppy at one such party, seen Troy himself weep immediately after; and heard the crashing of glass Poppy caused as she fell back against the Senior Porters' antique water-pitcher collection.

Those were the strange few years when everyone seemed lost and crazy, longing for the license of the youth they were losing that would have exonerated them and made their revels of the night before less depressing. The next morning, made their endeavors less desperate, and made the name of the person they sat beside in Junior year of high—such a seemingly short time ago—seem not at all as important to remember as it did seem. Those were the years at the beginning of the fifties; the short-lived shock-riddled time Jud thought of as the years A.D. —After Delia.

Now she was back. And Jud knew instinctively why Poppy had suddenly wanted to leave the table and dance, and not say any more than "Poor Chad" about the whole matter. Because Delia Benjamin's return would revive a great many memories, and Jud couldn't help recollecting that those were the exact same words Poppy had said when she had first mentioned Jack Chadwick to him.

She had said, "Poor Chad!" And not very much later, people in Bastrop were shaking their heads and saying, "Poor Poppy!"

Perhaps no one in Bastrop knew as well as Jud Forsythe did that Troy Porter's wife had a soft spot for a wounded bird; and perhaps no one in Bastrop knew as well as Poppy Porter did that Jud Forsythe had been one of the most wounded birds around, in the years he called "A.D."—the terribly painful years when he finally had had to resign himself to the fact he had really lost Dee not just to another man, but to his life; that she was gone out of his sight, he thought, for good; out of his mind, he believed, never.

What would it be like seeing her again? He looked up and a hundred and thirty-six-odd eyes winked at him.

PART THREE

*It was still raining when the stranger left Porter Drugs
and went back to the Wheel, where his car was parked.*

*He made a bed in the back seat, used a duffle bag filled
with clean shorts and shaving equipment for a pillow, and
shook out a lightweight topcoat for a blanket.*

*On the floor there was a stack of pamphlets, tied with
a string, which he cut with his silver penknife. He leafed
through them by the dim overhead light attached to the
roof of the car.*

*One in particular he liked. It was designed like a play-
bill. Across the front was printed in large letters:*

Could this be
YOUR FAIR LADY
in the near future?

*There was a picture of a white woman sitting on a Negro's
lap.*

*He turned the page. Another picture of a white woman,
kissing the Negro, their arms wrapped around one another.
The caption read:*

I've grown accustomed to your race
(It's second nature to me now.)

*He turned the page. There was a picture of white women
dancing rock 'n roll with Negroes.*

Above were the words:

I could have danced all night
(. . . spread my wings, and done a thousand things
I've never done before. . . .")

*On the fourth page there was a picture of Negro teen-
agers with sprung switch-blades in their hands, and wild
laughing faces with leering eyes, jumping over seats in a*

schoolroom where frightened whites cowered; Negroes pinning whites against the blackboard, cigarettes dangling from their mouths and gin bottles hanging in their hip pockets; Negroes gambling under the desks, dice rolling; and a white teacher with a tortured expression on her face, being bound to her chair with rope by Negroes.

The legend ran:

> *Wouldn't it be love-ah-ly!*
> *(All they want is a schoolroom somewhere. . .)*

The last page showed a long, tenement-crowded street, with Negroes shoving whites into the gutter; Negro faces laughing from windows high above; and Negroes lolling on front porches, while whites inside peeped fearfully from behind their curtains.

The words asked:

> *On the street where YOU live?*

The stranger tossed aside the pamphlet. There were countless others, some like it, some different.

Tomorrow he would distribute them, and the man he had met in the drugstore—Duboe Chandler—had promised to help him. That was luck—to come into a town cold and immediately win support. But *it's like me, too, the stranger thought; always been that way for me, always had a way with people, because I can read them, figure out their sick minds. Sick, sick, sick! Wanting to be well, and know I can help them; need me to tell them; that same way I told Chandler:*

Told him, "Look, Chandler, look at this," showed him the picture of that nigger banging on the white girl, "This is an actual photograph taken a few weeks ago up in Greenwich Village, New York City. Chandler, that nigger boy you see there—he's from down in Mobile, Chandler, a Southern jigaboo that went North and learned his wool head the word integration. *You know what that word means—integrate? You know what Webster's Dictionary says is the meaning of that word? Says it means to form into a whole, Chandler, to unite as one, Chandler. Just like that black ape's uniting as one with that white meat!"*

Told him: "How's it make you feel, Chandler, to see a

picture like this? Sure, makes you mad at that nigger; sure, Chandler, but I'm asking you for your candid opinion, Chandler. I'm talking man-to-man with you. There's another feeling too, happening to you right now because of that picture; and Chandler—" looking him deep in the eye, hand on his shoulder—"it's a sexual feeling. It is; you know it is! It's a feeling of lust, Chandler, and you know why? Because the whole subject of integration, of uniting the coons with the white race, which is the meaning of the word integration—and it's right in Webster's Dictionary, it's as basic as all that—why, that whole subject, Chandler, gets folks randy. Gets folks sexed up, Chandler. You got to admit it, and I've got to admit it." .. ..

Told him: "Ever had a yen for dark shagging Chandler? I'm asking you for your candid opinion on these subjects. You know as well as I do, before God, that the white man has had such a yen, has and does and always will. And, Chandler, it isn't good. I'm not preaching to you, fellow, I'm just telling you what both of us know. It sure as hell is not good at all when a white man gets a yen to shag a thick-lips, because it's an overwhelming, God-forgotten, Devil-driven black urge that he can't subdue in himself, that he can't throw off by lifting heavy furniture, or taking walks, or showers, or jacking-off—or none of it! It's an obsession that'll drive him out of his mind and set him to banging his head into cement if he doesn't get rid of it, and there's only one way he can get rid of it, Chandler, and that's by going the hell out and getting some colored gal and giving it to her!"

Told him: "Well, Chandler, I've got something scientific to tell you with regard to all this, and that is, that scientifically it's been proven, Chandler, actually proven that the white woman is capable of getting this yen herself. Just like the white man. The white woman is capable of getting this yen for a big buck of a nigger, hung like a bull and black as licorice, and that white woman in this very photograph—God help her somehow—is just such a woman. And Chandler, it's been scientifically proven that it never would have happened to this innocent, pitiful, sick, debased white woman you see here in this picture, if the black apes up North were controlled like they are in the South.

"It's a psychological fact," he told him, "that this yen

*is capable of starting up in women, Chandler, when nig-
gers are treated like white men."*

*Told him: "I've seen it happen to white women, wom-
en I knew, and yes, Chandler, women I respected, and
I wanted to die, and I wanted to cry, and Chandler, I
wanted to kill. I wanted to do murder, Chandler, actually
wanted to kill! It could drive a man to. Look at that
picture and think of the white girls you know; think of
your own woman, Chandler, and think how you'd feel if
that yen came over her. Think of that, Chandler, and
give me your candid opinion of how you'd feel. And think
of it hard and long, Chandler, because next Monday
morning could be the first step in that direction. It's just
basic, that's all. Just basic and sick. It's so sick I get sick
imagining it. God, Chandler, don't let such a thing happen
here in Bastrop, Alabama. Don't let it, Chandler. Help me
to stop it, because it's so sick!"*

*The stranger leaned back against the back seat and re-
membered the look in Duboe Chandler's eyes; remembered
the perspiration dotting his forehead and the way he had
perched on the stool at the soda fountain, cracking his
knuckles, saying, "A-yeah, a-yeah," in that dry, husky
tone, licking the corner of his parched lips, listening, listening.*

It was going to be easy. Had he ever doubted it?

*The stranger crossed his long legs, letting his foot swing
and idly kick the tall pile of white pamphlets. It was
cracker country, after all, filled and spilling with red-
necked peckerwoods and poor white mud-eaters. All they
needed was someone to tell them.*

The stranger thought of a poem he had written once:

> *Little, puny illiterati,*
> *Chump, dingbat, bone-top, block,*
> *Fool! You are of value*
> *As my tool.*
> *I can use you,*
> *And amuse you,*
> *And excuse you,*
> *(As a rule).*
> *Goof, woodhead, prize sap, dolt,*
> *Asses! You are the voice*
> *Of the masses.*

I shall need you
I shall lead you
I shall bleed you,
Lads and lasses.

What had his professor written across the top of the paper when he had handed it back to him? "Sounds like a bad attack of indigestion, Mr. Buddy."

Not everyone understood; not many did. But a few did; one in particular—Lenny Gold.

Lenny Gold had said once: "You make me afraid, Buddy. You scare the hell out of me!"

Lenny Gold understood, and before very long he'd have a lot of company.

3. *There's some here'bouts who favors being dissected, but I don't study dissection issues. I am busy occupying my mind in enough ways as is.*

—Ginny Towers

ONE of the ways Ginny Towers occupied her mind at the end of the work day, as she made her way down the bumpy dirt road to Puddin' Nelly in the dark, was to mull over every little thing that had happened up at Mister Jack's. In fact, life at Mister Jack's house not only occupied her mind all the time, more than any other thing, it kept her in a state of perpetual preoccupation. She'd go along doing whatever she was doing and thinking thoughts like: Must be dey had demselves some kinduv arg'ment las night, way they bangin' them coffee cups down on de saucers s'morning. Wonder what about?

Or, scrubbing the back porch in the afternoon: How come Miz Cass wear red so much de time? All de time wear red like dat. Seem silly, all de colors pick from, pick red time, time again.

And, down doing the marketing along Court Street: Mister Jack like his breakfuss coffee awright. Drink three, four, five cups de stuff. Nebber known nuther man liked his coffee s'well as Mister Jack. Don't see how he don't help but git the runs drinkin it cup after cup dat way, first thing the mornin'.

Then finishing up the dishes in the evening: Shame 'bout dat chile of ders. Eyes nebber seen de light. Poor blind kiddy, 'n dey jest carry right on like dey don't mind de least. 'N he hoppin' around like de whole world jest like him, laughin' 'n all.

Day in day out it was "up at Mister Jack's," whether she was remembering what had gone on when she was there, or whether she *was* there, and though everyone in Puddin' Nelly spoke of their bosses and their ladies, the consensus was that Ginny Lee Polk Ann Towers never could think up another subject. Turner Towers, her older brother —in Ginny's mind, an uppity nigger if there ever was one —used to try to explain to her that she ought to think of herself as an individual, as Ginny Lee Polk Ann Towers, age, early twenties; religion, Baptist; marital status, hopeful; and looks—Turner would always whistle in this part, wink, and cock an eyebrow, and try to tell her to stop thinking of herself simply as Mister Jack's hired girl. But since Turner married himself Doris Smith, and since he wasn't getting anywhere with his sister anyway, he gave up the subject. Duggan Allen, Ginny Lee's beau, a coal-black, lantern-jawed worker at Chandler's gin, never listened to what she said, so it didn't bother him one bit. And the only other person in Puddin' Nelly who had nothing against Ginny Lee's one and only topic of conversation was Grandma Towers, called Tappie, after the gnarled black cane she tapped around on, didn't need and was never without.

The highpoint of Tappie's day was when Ginny Lee came home after work and told her everything that had happened. Sometimes it wouldn't amount to anything, and sometimes it *would* amount to something, but Tappie hung on every word, chortling and grunting and uh-huhing, nodding her flocky white head, spitting into the pail at the side of the rocker, and murmuring, "Just like when I worked up to Mister Senior's;" or ". . . yea, sho, dat's de way allus;" and "Aw, naw, d'e do *dat!*"

There were the days of crisis, like the day little Master Johnny-Bob got an earache, and Ginny Lee hunted the fruit cellar, hands and knees, for a cockroach, took its head off, split it in half and was just pressing the juice into Master Johnny-Bob's ear when Miz Cass happened along and carried on as though Ginny were sticking nails in.

Screamed at Ginny Lee: "Don't you ever—*ever,* you hear—*never* try to doctor this child!"

Shouted: " Stupid, stupid, stupid! How could you have —" And then, "Just go on. Go on back to Puddin' Nelly now! Don't mind dinner. I'm too upset. No Ginny Lee, just *go!*"

Tappie, pressing her stricken granddaughter to her skinny, wizened body, had said, "Ain't yo fault, honey, 'at she don't know cockroach juice cure de earache. Cure de abscess in de ear too."

And there were the "nothing 'ceptional happened today" days, the ones when Ginny just recounted—fixed butter beans for dinner; had hell's time gettin Master Johnny-Bob in from the yard, gettin' more 'n more stubborn, not good either bein' blind *and* stubborn; thought Mister Jack looked tired; shoulda heard way he yelled at Miz Cass for leavin de top off de toothpaste tube, haw gee-Gawd, dough, she a sloppy liz, and dat's de truth—weren't for de fact ob my presence, she'd wipe de plates wid the cat's tail. Bought herself a new red sweater, need more red in dat house like rain need water—just recount; on and on—and Tappie listening; the two of them, lost dream-deep, deliciously in the land of "up at Mister Jack's."

That night as Ginny hurried down to Puddin' Nelly— late; way past eleven she'd baby-sat, with the vine-hung trees hanging with shadow hair and pointing shadow fingers in the hazy light of a quarter-moon cut by clouds, walking fast as she could with her corns showing off—that night was a crisis night, no doubt and emphatically. Much as they had tried to conceal it when they had come home, Ginny Lee read it on their faces in big print, and thought right when she saw them, just inside the door, with their wraps still on and their packages and newspapers still under their arms. She thought: Oat-oh, somethin's swimmin' in de trouble pond.

Then heard Mister Jack say in the kitchen: "I don't give a *good* cold shower in hell *what* you meant! Or who's back in town! Or what the stinking town thinks I think about integration—or the stinking town either, for that matter!"

"Shhh, Jack, honey. Ginny hasn't left yet . . . Listen, I

didn't mean anything. What am I supposed to do, look up and see you on your feet, with Delia Benjamin beside you, and suddenly find myself saying hello and how long you in town for; and then—pffft—end of scene. And what am I supposed to do? Not comment at all? Just say nothing at all about it, like she just walked up to our table any day of the week?"

Delia Benjamin! Yipe, *she* back! Ginny Lee took time gathering up her movie magazines, hanging up her apron, lingering in the hallway, and listening.

Heard: ". . . that at all, and now you know it! First you start on the editorial for the Monday edition, then make something out of the fact some old girl friend I forgot in the Year One comes back home and says hi."

"Will you keep it low, Jack? You know Ginny carries tales."

Thought: May carry tales, Miz Cass, but got better tales 'n the stupid dumb ones I hear in this place; got more to do wid my time 'n be blabbing 'bout you or anything to do wit you!

Heard: "Well tell her to get the hell on home then, and get off my neck, Cassie!"

And hustled then, hustled on out the door and halfway down the steps when Miz Cass yelled from the doorway: "Good night, Ginny, and thanks for sitting, hear?"

Called, "Night, Miz Cass!" Then stopped, called, "An' Miss Cass—you think I carries tales, you wrong! I got other things to study than tales, and I didn't hear nothin' in de first place!"

Miz Cass had sighed and let the screen door bang behind her; and Ginny Lee Polk Ann Towers had sucked in her breath, slapped her thigh with three back issues of *Motion Picture,* and sang:

> *Hot, daw, when I get in Il-li-nois*
> *I'm gon-na spread de news*
> *A-bout de Flo-ri-da boys.*
> *Shove it o-ver! Hey! Hey!*
> *Can't you line it?*

Puddin' Nelly was the Negro quarter in Bastrop, west of the courthouse and down by the tracks, below the brow of Love-Lucy Hill. There the shacks of the colored huddled together, hugging one another in shabby, resigned, unpainted squalor along nameless dirt streets; outhouses plugging the rears; broken rocking chairs and trash cartons and spring-popping white folks' hand-me-down couches squatting in the fronts.

It got its name from an old Negro who lived down there after slavery; said it was better living there than on the white man's land; said it was pretty nearly living, but not quite. He had pronounced it "puddin' nelly," and it stuck.

Love Lucy Hill was lined with dark water oaks and white sycamores, and off to one side was a city dump; and off to the other a stubble field with a yellow creek running through it. Ginny Lee lived creek-side in Puddin' Nelly, best side, and she was hurrying past the field when the man stepped out from behind the last water oak at the bottom of Love Lucy, and stood straddle-legged in her path.

She had been in the midst of thinking: ". . . course dat was all a long time 'go; still dey say Miz Delia 'n Mister Jack tought each odder were de moon, dey was so sweet-crazy for each odder. Still, Mister Jack seem right fond of Miz Cass—"

When she saw him—this man.

Ginny Lee was uncommonly pretty, a little girl with unusually long legs for someone her size, good legs that were thin but not sticks and showed finely molded ankles. And her breasts above the round hips and thin waist were large for someone her size, not in a way that gave her a top-heavy look, but a proud feminine look, when she remembered to hold her shoulders back and stand straight. Crabb Suggs, who always eyed her with a feverish, lecherous look spread across his fat, stubbled, red face, said she was angel-faced, and whore-proportioned. Ginny Lee, for her own part, was well satisfied with her looks, save for two things. She wished she weren't as light-colored as she was, because Duggan Allen claimed it made her look washed out and he wished she was black like he was so when they got married their kids would be; and claimed it worried him some. So it worried her. And the second thing was that her eyes needed glasses, and Duggan Allen said a four-eyes gave him the creeps; he didn't know why, but facts was facts; so that preyed on her mind, whenever it could find access.

Which it did that very night, the moment the man stepped out from behind the tree, and she stood there blinking and squinting to recognize him; thought for a moment it was Duggan kidding with her; feared for another moment it was Crabb Suggs, trying to corner her again, get her down with her arms pinned back, sit on her legs and say the dirty things while he got her blouse open and her skirt up.

"Duggan?" she asked.

He was Duggan's size, she thought; thought he was, but Lord, she couldn't see really. "Duggan?"

The man laughed.

She felt a little wave of relief; knew by the laugh it wasn't Suggs because Suggs had asthma and always wheezed when he laughed.

She said, "Who're you, huh?"

He didn't come any closer, and she had stopped in her tracks.

"I ain't that black nigger," he said. "You like it for me to be that black nigger, huh? A-yeah, a-yeah, you like it, wouldn't you?" He cracked his knuckles.

"What you want?" she said.

"I want to integrate you," he giggled. "Hah? Wha say?"

The clouds cut away from the quarter moon and she stepped closer. Then she recognized him.

She said, "Where *you* learn such a big word?"

"Not in no school niggers go to. You know niggers going to park their black asses right alongside white folks come Monday, up in the school, huh? Going to integrate," he pronounced every syllable of the word. "Going to unite as one, huh?"

"You off your stick t'night, sumpin?"

He walked closer, holding something in his hand—a photograph.

"Lookit here, Ginny Towers, see here."

"I can't."

"I'll scratch a match for you."

"Naw," she said. Then the flame lit up the photograph. "You filthy!"

"Want to desegregate with me, Ginny Towers?" He giggled and poked her stomach with his finger. "A-yeah, huh?"

"I'se sick of the subject of dissection," she said.

He reached out and gently tweaked her nipple. "I got my car at the dump," he said. " 'Member the ride we took a while back. 'Member how you asked? Asked for everything I did, din't yah, a-yeah!"

"Your car belong in de dump," she said. She was cupping her breast where he had pinched her, smoothing her hand up and down over it. "I didn't ask for nothin. You said I should ask."

"And you asked."

"Duggan hate you," she said. "Said you're meaner 'n anybody out dere at de gin. Said you're lazy."

"Tell Duggan that's why I'm boss." The man laughed again.

He took her hand. "C'mon," he said. "Let's integrate."

"Delia Benjamin's back in town," she said, as though she were saying it to herself, weighing things in the matter of their importance, thinking: I'll jest tell Tappie, well dere's someone in town we all ain't seen in some time, easy-like; just tell her gradual; den drop de bomb; haw-g, dog, Tappie gonna bust de gut.

The man said, "I know that. I saw her."

"Whyn't you ask her to tinnegrate?"

"Because of the fact we done already tinnegrated once before," he said, "and she's a dry lay. I got me better tail 'n that to hump."

"You a liar," Ginny Lee said. "She wouldn't look at you. She was Mister Jack's—"

"Don't start that," he said. "I tell you the truth. I had Free-Dee; had her when she was engaged to your Mister Jack."

"You don't dare swear on your hearing and eyesight," she said. She shook her hand away from his. "You a phony."

He stood in a solemn stance and raised his hand. "I swear on my hearing and I swear on my eyesight that I screwed Delia Benjamin."

"Don't—" she had tried to caution him in the middle of what he was saying, but he had gone right on. Now she regarded him carefully. "You gonna be deaf and blind?" she asked.

"I tell you," he said. "I tell you what I tell you."

"While Mister Jack was—while he was engaged?" But she already believed him. There wasn't much she believed she could be sure of about Duboe Chandler, but there was one thing: she could be sure he wouldn't swear that swear unless it were a fact he was attesting to.

"Come on," he said. "Car's down at the dump."

A new light hid in her lowered eyes. She was trying to piece things together.

He took her hand, "Coming? We ain't got all night to integrate, you know," he laughed.

She walked along with him and he slid his arm around her waist, let his hand stray up under her sweater. "Gawd damn, you're stacked, nigger!" he said, "I'm going to desegregate you all to hell!"

Ginny Lee Polk Ann Towers stepped over a clump of sticks, picked a long one out of the clump, and trailed it behind her in the dust.

She said, "Mister Jack nebber knew dat, did he, Dube?"

4. *I'm curious, that's all—that's what keeps me going. And most of the time I'm simply curious to see how much worse things can get.*

—Cass Chadwick

WHEN she first woke up she didn't remember it. The sun was streaming into the room, and as she squinted around, growing accustomed to daylight, she noticed the dirty fingerprints on the lemon-shaded wallpaper, and in her mind, blessed out Ginny for not wiping them clean. Then as always, when this came to her attention, she felt grief-sore and sorry for little Johnny-Bob, sickened by his sad necessity to feel his way along the walls, and momentarily she worried about him, tried to wonder over his future, and for the Lord only knows how many times, tortured her mind's eye with visions of her son being run over by a car he didn't see, falling down staircases he couldn't anticipate, tripping and bumping and being lost in a multitude of black places—with his small hands groping. And again, as always, it left her anxious and depressed, and more times than often, it was the way the day began; because she was an early waker, and once she did awaken, she was the kind who worried herself fully and finally awake.

Because she *didn't* remember the fight with Chad right

away, she dwelled on the more familiar anxieties, the routine ones—beginning with Johnny-Bob and ending with her dad's health. The latter was always accompanied by the determined vow to drive out and see John Beggsom before another day passed, a promise she made to herself time and time again, and seldom kept.

For the past four months a new anxiety had joined the familiar ones, namely Jack's position on integration in the Bastrop school system, and it was when she finally, sleepily, got around to that, during those slow seconds of gradual awakening, that she remembered. She had just pulled her arm from under the pillow on the huge double bed, where she had been lying on her stomach, her eyes studying the wall, when she looked down at her watch and saw the time, six twenty-five, and then recalled Chad's good night.

"I'm sick of you!" he had said. "I always was sick of your father, and now, finally, I'm sick of you! Is that clear enough for you?"

Then he had rolled over on his own side of the bed, and ten minutes later, commenced to snore.

Cassandra Chadwick did not cry herself to sleep after that, she pitied herself to sleep, curled into a fetal position beside him, but not touching him, she comforted one breast with her hand cupping it gently, and indulged in implacable brooding on the ironies of her plight that Friday night at the beginning of autumn.

There were many more in Bastrop besides herself who said the same thing she did about Chad's attitude on the Supreme Court ruling, the only difference being she said it to Jack, and they said it behind his back.

Said—like Senior Porter—"Trouble is, Jack's not a businessman, so he doesn't have to worry. But a merchant knows that whenever there's tension between the Nigraw and the white in a town as small as this, it's going to hurt business. And a merchant knows when a law like the school law is passed, it's just better to shut up about it."

Like Gus Chandler—"Trouble is, Chadwick don't work with niggers, don't know what makes them black apes tick. Now most niggers wouldn't 'uv paid no goddam attention to that law; woulda kept right on riding the orange bus over to Morrow to learn their wool heads how to spell cotton, and we wouldn't be violating the law none at all. But Chadwick's reminding 'em they don't have to cart their asses fifteen miles back and forth every day, and all they need is a little reminding. Just remind a lazy nigger he don't have to do something often enough, and pretty soon it sinks in that he don't have to do something. Chad's turned the *Citizen* into a goddam nigger memorandum!"

Like Arnold Belden—"Trouble is Chad's an outsider. He's from a big city in the midwest, and we're a small town in the Deep South. Integration is just another issue with him; with us, it's a tradition; and only someone born and raised down here can appreciate how we feel about traditions. When they're broken, we don't feel like sitting down on the back porch and reading in the evening newspaper that that's just the way the ball bounces sometimes, we better clap hands and grin."

Cassandra Chadwick had been sitting over a soda in Porter Drugs last night telling her husband what people were saying, and the fact that she had had to wait so long before she could had made it seem all the more important. It was something of an occasion—a turning point, really, when instead of turning away from a point in their marriage, they returned to an original point. For during the last few weeks, Cass had felt Chad come back, after a stolid summer's absence, when little things were magnified to giant proportions, and larger things minimized to seem of no importance at all. And they had grown apart from one another, not with the kind suddenness of a violent split, but in the more painful languid way which nagged and never burst.

She knew she could pinpoint the problem in two incidents, and in both matters she had been to blame; but in both, too, she had never been more herself. That was the wall between them.

The first had been at the beginning of June, out at the Legion picnic on the fairgrounds. It had been Jack's idea to take Johnny-Bob with them instead of leaving him with Ginny; and it had been the first time Johnny-Bob had played with any other children than the Scott twins from next door, or the Gaynor girl from down the street. After they had spread their blanket behind the long picnic table, facing the sandpile and slides and swings, Chad had stood up, taken Johnny-Bob by the hand, and walked him over there. Johnny-Bob was three, with a face peppered with wild brown freckles and cut across with a wide grin, rust-colored hair sweeping his brow. Some of the children playing in the sandpile were about his age; others were older—six, seven and eight.

Cass watched Chad say hi to them; watched them look up and then look at Johnny-Bob, all grins still—and imitating his father.

"Hi!" he said.

They answered him—some of them. Some kept on with their holes and castles, ignoring him.

Cass heard Chad say, "Want to sit down, John? There's sand there. There's a sand pile."

The child swung his hand free from Chad and squatted, touching the ground with his fingers, gradually sitting in the sand.

A small boy across from Johnny-Bob was watching carefully.

"Is there a pail?" Johnny-Bob asked.

"No, but you can dig a hole to China, can't you?" Chad knelt and began to help him.

Then the small boy spoke up. "What's wrong with him? Don't he see nothin'?"

Chad said, "Johnny's blind," in a matter-of-fact tone, continuing with his digging. Johnny-Bob scooped out some sand and let his fingers sift it, laughing.

"No kidding," the small boy said. "Can't he see my hand?" He leaned over and waved it at Johnny-Bob's face.

"Nope, he can't," Chad said.

By this time all the children were staring at Johnny-Bob; all had stopped what they were doing.

"Does he knew he's blind?" one girl asked.

"He knows the word blind, but it's hard for him to comprehend the meaning, because he never saw, like we do."

Johnny-Bob kept on digging.

"I could help him with that hole," the small boy said.

"See if he wants some," Chad grinned.

The small boy hesitated; then he hopped over beside Johnny-Bob. "Want some help?"

"Sure," Johnny-Bob answered, looked in the direction of the voice. Again the small boy waved his hand across his face, but Johnny-Bob looked away, back down at his digging. Then the boy put a tin shovel in his hand.

He said, "That's a shovel."

Someone from a swing nearby yelled at the boy, "Davis, c'mon and swing."

Chad was standing now, starting to walk away. He told Johnny-Bob, "I'll be right by. Give a holler if you want me, fellow."

"Okay," Johnny-Bob said.

Then the boy in the swing shouted again for Davis, and it all began.

Davis yelled, "Hey, c'mon and see the blind boy. He's blind, Simpson!"

Chad was walking toward Cass leisurely, lighting his pipe.

Cass sat forward, clutching her pearls at the neck of her silk blouse, watching what was happening. Other voices joined in at the sandpile: "C'mon and see the blind boy!" and before too long, a score of hopping, shouting, boys and girls of all sizes were crowded around Johnny-Bob. They were watching and pointing and calling—until suddenly Cass could stand it no longer. She leaped to her feet and ran—heedless of Chad's calling, "Cass, come on back here! Stop!" And when she reached the spot where her son was, surrounded by gaping eyes, she shoved them aside brusquely, yanked Johnny-Bob up by the arm, then stooping to pick him up, carried him away in her arms, tears rushing from her eyes.

Afterwards, when her moment of panic was over, after Chad had sent Johnny-Bob to return the tin shovel to the boy named Davis, after they had driven home silently on empty stomachs—Johnny-Bob had been let out to play in his own sandpile in his own backyard, and Cass had taken a book out on the sun porch to watch him—after long hours, when Chad finally came out and pulled up a hassock beside her, what he said made sense. That Johnny-Bob would have to face that sort of experience if he were to grow up in Bastrop and not off in some school for the blind; that he hadn't been hurt one bit by the shouts or the stares; only Cass had; and that Cass had to stop making so much of his blindness or she'd hurt him more than anyone ever could.

It made sense then; but even when she relived the moment, and remembered Johnny-Bob sitting there surrounded by children who stared at him as though he were a freak, heard their voices and the high cry, "He's blind; c'mon and see!" she could not keep the panic from beginning inside of her again, and a stricken feeling invariably flooded through her, stunning reason. . . .

The second offense had occurred in mid-July, that muggy afternoon when Chad was expecting a visit from an old Air Force buddy who was being driven up for the day from Mobile. About an hour before, Cass's father, John Beggsom, dropped by in his pickup on one of his rare surprise visits.

Chad hated John, and the feeling was mutual. When he and Cass had chosen the name John for their boy, it was because it was Chad's legal name, and he wanted a "Junior;" but it was also because he never remembered Cass's father carried the same name. Chad always called him "that one," "Beggsom," "that bastard," or "your father"—said like an oath of some kind.

Beggsom had been raised up in the Sand Hills, in the backwoods, in a dogtrot cabin. What brought him into Bastrop was a woman, Cass's mother, whom he'd bought shoelaces from in the five-and-dime, down on West Tennessee, when he was passing through on one of his sales trips. Beggsom had a still up in a place called Blue Pill and he sold the same moonshine he made, coming out of the hills every two months to do it. When he fell for Angie Carmer, he gave up the still, used the profits from it, and years of savings, to buy a gas pump and a shed, and moved to the outskirts of Bastrop.

Beggsom hated three things most in this life—the law, the niggers, and the Lord—in that order. He was a medium-sized, square-built, unkempt fellow with a backwoods accent and a backwoods sense of humor that bordered on the vulgar; but he loved his own as violently as he hated what wasn't his, and few people ever forgot the story of the night Angie Beggsom died in childbirth. It was known all over Bastrop that mere seconds after Doctor Walker lifted Cass from between her dying mother's legs, John Beggsom drank a quart of whisky, one tumblerful after the other, in the dark of his front room, scowling and shouting at the four walls because he had loved her in a crazy way, and when—near dawn—a neighbor came to try to convince old John that he should sleep, Cass's father was found on his knees on the linoleum in the kitchen, his big arms smashing through the air in fast, powerful waves, killing house ants with a hammer, crying like a baby.

If John Beggsom loved his own with an emotion too powerful for reason to penetrate and tame, his daughter loved *her* own with an emotion unchanged by its frequent exposure to reason. Whenever Chad began one of his tirades on Beggsom, Cass consoled herself with the thought that Chad had never known "close" family and checked her impulses to get up and holler herself red in the face at him, because most everything he said about her father was right; but she never said she liked John Beggsom. She loved him; that was something else.

So when Chad said, "Get your old man out of here before Tim comes. He didn't fight a war to come back crippled and meet *his* kind," Cass stuck to her guns. She said she wouldn't make him go, she couldn't, and Chad better not say one dang-dong word to him, or she'd go with him. She said Tim should understand he was a poor stupid old man, and she said she'd warn Beggsom not to say anything about the law or the niggers or the Lord. And it was while she was arguing with Jack just inside the screen door— with old John out in back under the crab tree—that a horn honked and Tim Ottley was there.

He was in a wheelchair, paralyzed from the waist down and without the use of his right arm; and there was a silver plate encased somewhere under the head of sparse brown hair. His round, sunk-in eyes were a matching brown, and solemn and wondering; and he talked in a slow, low tone, pausing for seconds between words, thinking over everything he had to say. He had been in hospitals for years; in rehabilitation homes for more years; and ultimately he had come back to Mobile, thin-haunted and search-worn. Most of what he had to say concerned his years of searching for some answer to himself and what he would do with that broken self, and about his decision to become a Presbyterian minister. He spoke of God's work and God's grace and the faith, and all through it, Cass held her breath, and Chad's eyes darted nervously from Beggsom back to Tim Ottley.

Beggsom had been shifting his legs in the wicker chair set on the lawn, rubbing his chin with his stubby fingers, and fidgeting with a loose button on his short-sleeved blue shirt, the front of it stained with coffee, he'd spilled there. He had listened to Ottley, and nodded with his lips pressed together, and he had scratched his ear periodically and frowned, as though he were thinking over everything that was being said.

Then what both Cass and Chad were afraid would happen, did happen—happened above Chad's protests and with Tim Ottley's pale-faced, overpolite encouragement.

"Of course we want to hear the joke," Ottley had said.

"It has to do with God," Beggsom drawled, "and with a young feller like yourself, and as I'm to swear it now, it's a true story I was witness to, back in the hills in the middle twenties, when you was only a gleam in your daddy's eye."

"Papa," Cass attempted, "maybe Tim would rather just talk with—"

But Ottley said again "No, let's hear it, Mr. Beggsom."

John Beggsom crossed and recrossed his legs, took a deep breath, and then said: "Happened at one of these here back-brush holyings. Old parson was preaching like a cow in heat, and the congregation was rolling around, yipping and kicking up straw. Parson got done and said 'twas the hour for testifying, and after a coupla folks got up and told what the Lord done for 'em, the parson called on a countryside cripple to rise up and say what the Lord done for him.

"Well, sir—" Beggsom drew another deep breath and rubbed his cheek—"Brother Fink, 'at was the cripple's name, was one of these paralytics, like yourself, with his limbs all twisted like snakes coiling around one 'nother, going every which way. When the parson asked him to rise up and testify, Brother Fink rose, jerking and knocking like a new Ford on an old country road, trying to get his chin a bare inch from his chest, and trying to coordinate his lagging limbs. Everybody at the holying got quiet to see what he'd have to say and hear him testify." Beggsom straightened himself in the wicker chair.

" 'Well, sir—' Brother Fink paused a bit, eyeing his audience, and then he began to shrill—'You wants to know what the Lord done for me, he begins. Well, I'll tell you. He jest blamed near ruint me!' "

Beggsom leaned back in the wicker chair, rocking it on two legs and laughing uproariously. Cass looked across at Tim Ottley. His leps trembled in a desperate attempt to smile, but his face was ashen, and unforgiving.

Then Chad announced simply, "You'll have to leave now, Beggsom."

Oblivious to anything he might have done wrong, for John Beggsom was as insensitive as an old snapping-turtle, his weathered, red-nosed face lost its smile wrinkles, and his eyes, of the dull clearness of cooling lard, wondered.

"What'd I do?" he asked his daughter, for no matter how old Beggsom hated Chad, he always tried to be amiable when he called on them, to *show* Chad, for his "little girl."

Chad said, "Just go!"

And Cass—witness to the mute injury that spread across the ignorant, time-worn face, alert to the blow at her father's stubborn pride, now shattered and crushed—rushed to his defense.

"Don't you dare talk to Papa that way!"

As a result of what followed then, it was Tim Ottley who left, pushing the rubber wheels of his chair with fierce determination toward the car where the Negro driver waited, protesting that he really did have someone else to see in the same county, and swearing it honest to God didn't matter at all, that he knew it was just a joke; that he hated to be the cause of a fight; that he'd sure enough keep in touch, and when, hey, were they gonna be down Mobile way; stop in; don't forget, bye, and look, don't think about it another minute, hear?

Constantly during the age-long summer, Chad made reference to those two incidents, and each time it was the springboard to another fight. With the curious false modesty that overcomes a man and woman who sleep in the same bed, but who no longer seek the adjacent flesh for comfort, or love, or lust, Jack began wearing pajama bottoms, instead of sleeping in the raw as he always had, and Cass wore simple cotton pajamas, instead of silk and nylon negligees. Mealtime was no longer a time for discussing the *Citizen,* for they rarely discussed anything anymore, and on weekend nights, they began to see a lot of bad movies.

It was a hot, boring summer of discontent, but then—miraculously, in the unrealized, creeping slow way the seasons change and are all at once just there—it was over. Suddenly it was the end of summer and the beginning of fall, and it was heralded in the high groan of ecstasy as Cass received him again, and at last; and things were new for it, and better, and back to normal. Anyway, she had thought they were; she had been sure, or she would never have attempted last night to tell him what she thought he should know—what folks were saying, and what she had been thinking, as well, about the editorials.

Then, the irony, coming like the quick snap of a wrist before the palm met the face—Delia Benjamin standing there before them in Porter Drugs' beguiling and breathless with charm, the piquant aroma of some expensive perfume pervading the moment; and then, the slap in the face—as one gloved finger leaned on Jack's sleeve, and the husky tone purred: "Chad, you're doing a great job with the *Citizen*. I read two back issues in the car coming from Baldwin," pausing, smiling, the finger slipped from his sleeve to fondle the infinitesimal gold lapel watch on her suit, "In all sincerity, Chad, I was *immensely* impressed. Particularly by the editorials." Another pause; another smile, "Wonderful, Chad!"

Cass could feel her husband stir·beside her in the big bed. Often in the sleepy beginning of morning Chad turned toward her, the red hair rumpled, eyes not yet fully open, hands reaching for her, touching her fondly in the soft and secret places, murmuring drowsily before he turned back to the big, short, second sleep of morning; but now he only flattened out on his stomach, stuck his arms up under the pillow, sighed and was still again.

"I'm sick of you!" he had said last night.

Cass ran her hand along her pajama bottoms, from the waist to the stomach, down to where her legs began, to the part of her Chad called Mrs. Mine.

"He's fed up, Mrs. M.," she said to herself. "He's had us."

And it depressed her all the more to know that in three days she would be thirty.

5.   *Deel married me because she liked herself*
when she was with me, and because
she really hated herself.

—*Maurice Granger*

Out where U.S. 11 crossed State 1, a quarter of a mile from Bastrop, there was a drop in the land, where for a few acres a miniature valley ran, which was embraced by Judas trees and cedars, black gums and maples, and which was hard to see from the road. It was called the Dip, and that morning some minutes after seven, it was the only place where Delia Benjamin was sure she could be alone.

One of the things she missed about New York was the fact that you could take a solitary walk there without being considered lonely, troubled, or eccentric, even if you were all three; and that it wouldn't matter the time of day or night.

That and the myriad other facets of big-city life that created the blessed state of anonymity, Dee missed even more than she had imagined she would, but the one thing she missed most, which she had been too perceptive to underestimate, was Maury's presence.

In the pocket of her silk dress was the letter she had written him last night, the kind of letter she would ordinarily have ripped to shreds immediately after writing— long pages of sordid and depressing confessions and recantations—a pitiful attempt to reconstruct something that had been dilapidated to begin with—their "relationship," as Dr. Mannerheim would put it, but to Dee, simply, the awful mess of their marriage, and its nerve-naked aftermath.

There was a smell of burning brush in the air, goldenrod lit the wiregrass, and there was little sound except for the crunch of acorns underfoot, or the distant rumble of tobacco loads up on the road, bound for market under faded quilts. Dee fingered the corners of the thick envelope and thought that she was a far cry from analysts' couches, Miltown and what Maury called get-it-out-of-our-system-nightcaps, but here, she thought, was where the roots wept; here, was the beginning of it all.

And she had not wanted to come back. That afternoon a week ago, when she had sat at the tiny square table in the rear of the cocktail lounge at the Gotham, sickened already by the fact that he was late, when he was *always* on time, she had still clung to the hope he would not say something like: "Dee, I think it'll do you good," when she had said, after he apologized (offering no excuse—God, Maury!), seated himself and ordered the familiar J. & B.— neat, "I've been thinking, Maury—" she had watched his eyes closely— "that I'll leave town—" no flicker of emotion — "that I'll go back to Bastrop—" still none— "for good!"

A frown had creased his forehead—for only a second.

And then, the sentencing. For she had thought of his re-action to the news as a sentence: "you, Deel, my darling, beautiful, neurotic, ex, are condemned to life in Bastrop." Then, the conditioned reflex of the psychiatrist's failure, made her think: A sentence, Delia? Like Judge Benjamin sentenced people? Is Maury, the father, punishing you again for being naughty?

"What are you smiling at?" Maury had asked, watching her.

"I'm thinking of Pavlov's dog."

"Oh, conditioned reflexes and all, ah?"

"No," she had said, "I'm thinking of the poor goddam dog. I bet there's not a soul around who even remembers his name."

"Identifying again, ah darling?" Maury licked a pretzel. "The search for immortality," he sighed, "the fear of death. Deel, Deel, it'll be lonesome without you."

It was that easy for him. Or was it?

Last night as Dee had set at the desk in the living room, ancestral portraits staring at her from every angle in the room, the antique highboy stopping in the corner near where the grandfather clock chimed the quarter-hour—past midnight—she had thought she must have misinter-preted that meeting. She had tried to relive it through Maury's eyes; to imagine how *he* had felt, he who had begged her once never to leave him. "Never, no matter what I say or how I act, Deel, never even if I tell you to go. Promise to stay. Say it!"

And while she had shouted back at her mother, "No, Mama, I'm not coming to bed for a while. Now hush, and don't worry," she had remembered that side to Maury—that everything had to be said. He always called it his com-pulsion.

All right, Maur, she thought, all right, there's more, buckets more, darling. Is that it? You want to hear every-thing? Will *that* do it? Because something is going to have to!

As quietly as she could, she had gone upstairs to her room, lifted the pigskin suitcase onto the folding luggage rack, at the foot of the canopied bed, and from under the slips and bras and panties, taken out the fifth of J. & B. she had packed. A nightcap with Maur, she had thought, like old times; prepare the patient for surgery; it is the hour of the guts, and I'm going to spill mine.

She was carrying the bottle by the neck when she collided with Flo Benjamin in the hallway. Her mother was wrapped in a faded pink robe over the gray nightie—hair in a net, lips pursed, her bridgework back in her room in a tumbler of water.

"Liquor, Delia?" she said.

"Mama, I'm going to have one nightcap. Puts me to sleep, Mama."

"I'm sick about it, Delia. A daughter of mine drinking alone at midnight. Gaw, Delia, I'm just sick in bed about it!"

"Mama, don't be silly," Dee passed by her, starting down the spiral staircase with its Chinese Chippendale woodwork. "Don't worry so. It's not necessary."

Mrs. Benjamin had whined: "It was meetin' Chad like that, so sudden 'n all. Now it's driving you to sit up till morning, drinking. Gaw, Delia, don't let him do that to you hear?"

As Delia rounded the corner on the way to the kitchen she heard her mother call: "He's not half so well thought of as you may think, Delia. More than one say he's a Nig-raw-lover. He's not worth sittin' up past dawn swillin' whiskey over. You listen to your mother."

In the kitchen, as Dee broke ice from the rubber tray, she remembered that evening in Paris, the day of her twenty-fifth birthday. Maur had wanted everything to be perfect; he had made arrangements way in advance. She had read in a travel guide of Laperouse, a restaurant on the Quai Voltaire, and Maur had made reservations there—but they had driven up and down every crazy, twisting street on the Left Bank, because Maur had wanted to surprise her, and he had given only the address to the taxi driver, and the old man could not understand his French. So hours from the time they left the hotel—Dee, dressed in net and satin, frshly made up and beautiful—the cab had reached the restaurant, and, perspiring from the heat, dust-blown and exhausted, they had made their entrance. The second surprise Maur had planned was a room all to themselves—instead of eating in the elegance and excitement of the main dining room, they were to be cooped up in a tiny cubicle

alone and suffocating. And on the winding staircase that
led to it, Dee broke a heel and turned an ankle. When they
were finally back to the hotel—Dee forcing rage back—
Maury made the nightcaps in the room—made them the
way he always did—one small, melting cube, to one tall
glass of whiskey and soda. And Dee had sat across from him
on the big iron bed and thought: Your drinks are the same
way you are, limp and feckless; thought it so indignantly
and vindictively that when she got to her feet and snapped:
"I need more ice!" Maur had looked up at her and answered quietly, "I know what you mean, Deel, I know
what you're telling me."

Even as he was saying it, the boy appeared at the door
with the cable. The judge was dead. He had been buried
that same day.

Carrying her drink from the kitchen back to the living
room, Dee made a mental note: Juan les Pins, summer '52,
the English squash player. And another: Florence, same
summer, the man—Emile? Emilio?—from the Pitti Palace.
All right, Maur—everything will be spelled out in capital
letters for you. Will that help? As she sat down at the rosewood desk with the Scotch in one hand and a ball point
pen in the other, she believed it would help, the way the
heart-lonely and, tired-past-midnight, is slow to perceive
what next morning it knows is ridiculous.

Still, Dee had reread the letter an hour ago, sealed it, and
carried it with her on the walk; perhaps merely to make
certain that Flo Benjamin would not have access to it,
before it was burned or torn up and destroyed; and perhaps
because for some little hour Dee wanted to believe she
carried in the pocket of her dress an answer to Maury and
to her, that would make it all right again in some swift and
sudden metamorphosis—the way it used to happen when,
injured at play, she ran to the judge for the magic promise:
"We'll make it all better, Dee-Dee, we'll make it all right
again."

The sun was rising higher in the sky over Bastrop now,
and off in the distance a red fox struck out for the brown
hills. Dee found a log near a black gum, sat and fished in
her bucket bag for a cigarette. She tapped it on her long
red nail, and thought of the way Maur would have had a
match lit by now, would have reached his long arm across

to give her the flame. Then suddenly from behind her she felt an arm extended, saw a silver identification bracelet on a thin white wrist, and a flame flickering from a bullet-shaped lighter.

"It's nice to see you again," a voice said.

PART FOUR

It was nearly seven in the morning and the Chevy was going too fast for one that didn't know the country. Like its driver, it was from the North. a city car used to straight paved controled-speed highways, and the twists and snags of State 1 sent it dizzily through the Red Hills, like some crazy moonshiner from over in the mountains, too jug-bitten to find the worn and familiar patch back to the holler.

Since dawn the stranger had been driving through the thin pines and past the vine-hung woods of Tate County, by the festering swamps and restless yellow rivers, hardly look-ing at what there was to see around him, not even disgusted, as some strangers get, at the dust the car kicked up, not even aware of the noise that stack of pamphlets made in the back seat as they slapped the leather on the turns.

The radio in the '45 Chevy was tuned into WJLD over in Birmingham, to Gospel Jubilee Records, but Richard Buddy wasn't aware of that either. He just sat driving, his face stone set with the frown on his forehead below the carefully combed straight black hair, his brown eyes intent on his thoughts, mouth full and firm, lips tightened a little the way a man's will when he's concentrating on some-thing, and small square hands gripping the steering wheel tightly.

All night down at the Wheel he had tossed and turned on his makeshift bed in the rear of the car, alternately plagued and teased by mocking and provocative dreams, which danced across his mind's screen in one dizzy reel after the other. In one his hand had suddenly started turn-ing black as a nigger's while he was making a speech against desegregation, and when he had tried to hide it in his pants pocket, it wouldn't fit. He had awakened pound-ing his side with his fist. In another a beautiful woman—who was she? where had he seen her before? he searched his waking mind in vain—had opened the car door, touched his shoulder gently and announced, "You have won a prize. Mr. Buddy, you have won a prize for—" and then wild cheering and applauding crowds drowned out her words, and she was kissing him while he wondered why he had won the prize—and he had awakened suddenly with a keen sense of frustration, still trying vainly to hear the words after "prize for—" . . . .

His night was a patchwork of quick, queer, unconsummated dramas, which left him with an empty feeling in the pit of his stomach, and made him wish morning would come soon. And even before morning did come he had sat up, rubbed his eyes, worried and thought and planned over the problem he faced, climbed out of the car and urinated against the fender countless times—his bladder always belied his ostensible calm—and cleaned under his fingernails, where there was no dirt, where there never was, with his silver penknife. Until finally he had decided to drive anywhere, fast until morning came.

Even now his whole attention was on the problem; it seemed that no time of day, no road, no slapping of pamphlets in the back seat, no Jubilee singing—nothing—could take his mind from it. But then something did.

It was standing right smack in his path, in the spot of the newly risen sun, on the road's center line, and Richard Buddy came close to mowing it down. He punched his brake pedal with his well-polished loafer and the Chevy whined to an abrupt stop. Winding down the window, Buddy looked out at a man, a big fellow, even taller than himself, but not much older. Buddy placed him in the middle thirties. For some reason he always thought of how old a person was. At twenty-nine it seemed important to him, because he was all too aware of the fact that in a few years he would not be Richard Buddy, a young man of promise. In his own mind he framed it that he would be, in a few years, somebody or nobody. So in the beginning when he met people, he tried to size them up in his mind, as to their potential, their failure, or success. Those —like Duboe Chandler, the man he had met back in the drugstore last night—who seemed never to have had any potential, therefore had neither chance of success of any real sort, or of failure, were specks to Buddy. He was incapable of taking them seriously, or caring about them at all, except during the little hour of their importance to him. In his book they were merely punctuation marks.

This fellow was one of them, Buddy decided, before he had even spoken to him. A big hunk in a thread-bare light-

weight sweater, with an olive-green fatigue hat pulled over his no-color hair, smoking a stubby black pipe. A speck— out stopping cars on a bad state road, probably not a quarter in his pants. At that thought, Buddy remembered with considerable depression that he himself had slightly under eight dollars with him in Alabama—$50 back in the Manhattan Savings—and then, uneasily, Buddy thought of the fact that he was out in the middle of nowhere, in strange country, and some bums rolled a man for even less than eight dollars. He touched the button lock on his door and thought of rolling the window back up, but the big fellow was leaning his arm on top the glass now, grin- ning at Buddy.

"You were coming at me like you were set on killing me," he said.

"I didn't even see you."

"I started out for a little hike this morning and hiked myself about four miles farther than I'd counted on. Not too proud to beg a ride."

"I'm going to Bastrop," Buddy answered, trying to measure in his mind the gain in picking up this fellow. He seemed to be fairly well spoken, for a Southerner, but half the time Richard Buddy never could decide, when he was South, whether he was talking to a literate or an illiterate; sometimes they all sounded like niggers.

But before Buddy decided for or against the hitchhiker, the fellow had taken his words as an invitation; smiled, "Fine, I'm going there myself," and passed by the front of the Chevy, and opened the door on Buddy's other side.

"So you're going to Bastrop?" he said, getting in, "What brings you our way?"

Buddy'd been wrong about the no-color hair. The man took off his cap and passed his hand over his head as he settled, and Buddy saw the great shock of yellow hair, gold even in the faint light, and neatly parted. He had an im- pressive look from his heavy high-top boots to his rugged, strong-jawed countenance. Seeing him fumble for a light for his pipe, Buddy gave him one from his lighter, and looked him over. Thirty-four or thirty-five, a morning's stubble on his chin, big shoulders and huge white hands; bright, alert eyes—green, or blue?—and a wide mouth with good white teeth. Seemed all right, Buddy guessed; some hick from back country.

"Thanks." The man grinned again. Then repeated his question. "What brings you to Bastrop?"

"You live there, or near there?" Buddy asked. If he didn't Buddy didn't want to go into it. Not in detail. It took too much out of him, and he'd have enough to do in a few hours.

"I live in Bastrop," the man said.

"Oh? Well—good!"

"Are you on business of some sort, or visiting?"

"I'm doing a little of both," Buddy said, pleased that he'd picked the fellow up now; looked like the kind he wanted. "I'm visiting you people because of something that's my business and your business—everybody's business, really." He looked at the fellow and the man nodded encouragement.

"I'm interested in the segregation issue, or as some people put it, the desegregation issue."

Glancing at his rider, Buddy saw the expressionless face, the lips clamped over the stem of the black pipe, smoke spiraling up to the roof of the car, making it stuffy. Buddy didn't smoke and didn't approve of people who had that habit, considering it a weakness; but he carried the lighter to give lights. Good gimmick.

"How does Bastrop figure?" the man said finally, feeling Buddy's surveillance.

"You know what's happening Monday, don't you? The niggers are going to school in Bastrop. They're not going over to their own school in Morrow any more! They're going to school in Bastrop," Buddy said, and added emphatically, "with whites."

"Ummm-hmmm." The big fellow sucked his pipe. "We all know that."

Buddy was frustrated at this reaction, but he knew how to get these crackers' shackles up. Said, "Of course, that means mixing the races, inter-racial marriages and all. Niggers think they're privileged to marry white girls."

"Even so," the big fellow said, "even if that were true, how many white girls you think would consent?"

"Let me tell you something," Buddy said. "I come from up North and I've seen how this thing works. You'd be surprised what happens when you give the nigger that inch. He puts on a necktie and takes a bath just like you and me, and before you know it some little white girl who's been

reading too much Freud just simply doesn't see color any more. Ever think of that?"

"A girl ignorant enough to marry a man that bathes with his necktie on can't pick and choose," the man chuckled.

Buddy controlled a sudden surge of anger which seemed to well up in him. It was a vague form of the fury he felt when he lived in the Village, rooming with Lennie Gold, and Lennie would jump like a cat for a clothes moth on every single little slip of the tongue; snicker and smirk at him rocking his heels with his hands thrust in, his trouser pockets making some supercilious comment like "Very interesting, Richard. You just said I can't fate, instead of I can't fake. Are you concerned with your fate, my boy? Worried you're not making out as you should?" People who doted on twisting other people's words just to have a second's tee-hee, and people who waited with their hands halfway to their mouths for someone to make a mistake when he was saying something important—people like that were small. Small, and sick.

Buddy said coolly, "I don't think you understand the implications behind what's about to happen in your town on Monday."

"I understand one thing. A law's been passed."

"I hope you're not a nigger-lover." Buddy glanced at him, as though to point a finger of suspicion, hoping the fellow would take notice and vehemently deny any such thing. But he only sighed, taking his pipe from his mouth. Holding it, he said, "I'm not a Nigraw one-way-or-the-otherer, but a law's been passed. That's all."

"A damn fool law!" Buddy said. "A law you can change by force! By ignoring a law that leads to niggers and whites walking arm in arm, hand in hand—and mister, that's where this law leads. Do you like that idea?"

"I think I ought to respect the law," the man said.

"I wouldn't call you a typical Southerner," Buddy said in a sarcastic tone.

The man didn't notice. He said, "And you?"

"The whole nation's watching Bastrop, Alabama, this week," Buddy said; thinking God damn, he's got me started; now I got to stop and take a leak; "but I guess you're only concerned with yourself."

"Sometimes that's a full-time job," the man smiled. "Are you affiliated with some organization?"

"I'm going to pull over a second," Buddy said, "and take a leak. No, I'm a private citizen like yourself."

"From up North?"

"New York City."

"And you came all the way down here to Bastrop because the Nigraws are going to school Monday?"

"Because they're going to school with the whites," Buddy said. "Where will I pull over. Here?"

"Seems like a long way to come for trouble. You can pull in just ahead there, where State crosses Eleven. You'll want to go on down Eleven, takes you right into Bastrop."

Buddy said emphatically, "It was!" Then he noticed the man pointing ahead of him.

"Right down the side of this road, there's a dip. You can run down there. Be out of sight. I'll walk from here. It isn't far."

"Why don't you wait?" Buddy said, easing his foot down on the pedal, letting the motor run as the car stopped, "I'm only going to take a leak. Be a minute."

But the big fellow got out on his side and said, "I appreciate the lift."

"Why don't you come down to the courthouse at noon?" Buddy said. "I intend to give a little talk."

Buddy's rider waved. "I might at that," he said. Then he waved again, unsmiling, and went.

Going down the slope, toward the cluster of Judas trees and blackgums, Richard Buddy saw someone—a girl with short black hair—the girl, he thought with some slow amazement, who had given him the prize in last night's dream. She was standing there alone in the clearing by a log—as real as life.

Then he remembered that yesterday he had nearly collided with her at the drugstore.

6.

"Senior, do you think our boy's happy?"
—Gay Porter

W HY do you ask that?" Senior Porter had said, spooning up the sweet milk gravy at breakfast that morning. "Seems happy, don't he? Got everything he wants, I'd imagine."

But Gay Porter was always asking that—always—since Troy was born on the day President Harding died, that sizzling summer she won first in jellies and fourth in cakes at the Tri-County fair.

She asked the question, and then she answered it: "Law, I don't know, Senior. Poppy always dragging her folks along with them on their nights out." Answered it that way or some other way, but always in a way that hid —even from herself—the secret disappointment she harbored over the fact that her son had seldom needed her for comforting; that she had rarely had occasion to "take up for him" in the face of criticism; and that his life, unlike his father's, and unlike Gay's own daddy's, had been a relatively mild and blameless one. Only when he had gone through what Mrs. Porter thought of as, "that period with Poppy" before their marriage, had he ever really seemed confused, or reckless, or "in trouble." And then, Mrs. Senior Porter had felt morbidly depressed over Troy's position in the matter, because to her mind a man did not snivel after another man's girl. A man played the field, and he whored, he was always hard to get, and never wholly captive, but he did not make a fool of himself over a young lady who didn't return his affection. And in the rare cases when a man *did*, it ended tragically; and he almost never married her. He almost always married someone else, and the "affair" became something of a family legend—the dark-lady-in-daddy's-past sort of legend.

Senior Porter had pulled his napkin out of his vest, tossed it beside his bowl, and sighed, "Well, now, Gay—Troy's always liked the Beldens. Don't suppose he minds at all Poppy's dragging them along: Putting it in that understated way; because neither Gay nor Senior wanted to accept fully the Judas truth that their son was more taken by Poppy's folks than his own.

After he had breakfasted, Senior had gone off into the back yard to play with his son's children before going down to the drugstore for the day, and Gay had sat at the table in her rose-colored wrapper, stirring her second cup of tea, listening to the squeals of little Pryce and May B. as Senior romped under the plum bushes with them, and studying the clock, that had belonged to her great Uncle Colin and that now rested on the antique round table in the corner. It was eight o'clock, and Poppy had promised to come by eight to pick up the children. But Poppy was careless about so many things.

Gay Porter was not careless. She was a handsome white-haired woman with every pin in place. Married thirty-seven years to Senior, she'd never once let him see her with her teeth out; never once appeared before him with rags in her hair or grease on her face; and always remembered to touch her ear lobe with some soft scent before he came home in the evening, when she got up in the morning, and at bedtime.

He used to say—back in the love-ripe, tremble-sighing years of not-married-long: "Oh, God-Lord, God-Lord, my darling, I can remember the way you smell *right now,* sometimes when I'm in the midst of filling a prescription, and I ache around my groin, and I feel like coming on home and business be gone-dogged!"

And now he said: "Honey, you still wear that sweet-smelling stuff, don't you? S'nice."

And in between then and now, there was enough living to make the now seem enough and more, for any man to tell his wife in bed.

For Gay Porter had married Senior, neck-deep, candy-ankle in love with him, and Senior was a good catch on both sides of his family and in looks and charm as well. She had known him to be wild with tender passion for her and rough with unpolished lust for her; and the night Troy was born, she'd known too that he'd been down in Selma with Lynn-Ann Allston, a girl ten years younger than himself, from over in Baldwin, where he'd been going for some seven months to carry on an affair. She'd held him and rocked him like a baby in her arms when Troy's little sister, May-Belle got killed by a school bus; and one night after a druggist convention when he came home from New York City with lipstick-covered handkerchiefs and a new word, "call-girl," she'd heaved a ship-shaped paperweight at him, hit him in the head, and scarred him. Together they had loved, budgeted, fought, splurged, laughed, prayed, gossiped, and traveled as far north as Boston, as far South as Miami, and as far West as Ohio. Their marriage had proved successfully exciting. And if Gay had to admit that her son's marriage was equally successful, she would never see anything exciting about it.

What had ever excited Troy about Poppy in the first

place, Mrs. Porter simply could not fathom try as she might.

She sat there sipping her coffee, worrying it all, when she heard the back screen door slam, and the snap of the radio's button in the kitchen. Sometimes she wondered if Doris ever listened to the music that played over the radio from the time she arrived in the morning. to the time she left in the evening, or if the colored girl just kept the radio on to shut out the rest of the world while she was working. Sometimes Mrs. Senior Porter was impatient with the thought that Doris Towers was actually disinterested in the personal life of the Porters, that she was unlike other help in that she seemed more aloof and withdrawn. For some perverse reason it annoyed Gay to believe that Doris didn't even "carry tales" back to Puddin' Nelly about Senior and her; that she didn't listen to conversations or rummage through private things, and God knows she was a readin' nigger too, could both read and write. Mrs. Porter wasn't sure, but she thought she'd heard somewhere that the colored girl had even gone to college down in Selma.

Probably the thing that irritated Gay Porter most about Doris Towers was the thought she·had the moment the girl came through the kitchen door into the dining room. Thought: Gaw, she *is* a beauty—even in that tacky white maid's dress.

"Do you want me to clear now?" the girl said.

Gay Porter believed the story that had circulated about a year ago. Crabb Suggs had hidden in the dark down near Love Lucy Hill one night, people said, and when Doris Towers came from Chadwicks', where she used to work, Crabb Suggs had knocked her down and raped her. Senior always told it that Suggs had knocked her down and knocked her up, and Turner Towers had gotten into such a swivet over it he'd actually tried to bring Suggs to trial. He'd gotten up a signed petition saying Suggs was always hanging around Love Lucy Hill at night waiting for the colored girls, and he'd tried to get the law to prosecute Suggs.

Crabb said at the time that the scratches on his face were from some damn fool cat he'd tried to get out of the back of his car when he was over in the next county fishing—that same night—and Duboe Chandler and John

Beggsom swore they were with Crabb, even brought a cat's carcass in to the sheriff and said they'd had to shoot the critter out of the car.

People said Deacon Phillips, the nigger minister, saw to it Doris Towers got aborted over in the nigger clinic at Morrow; and some said Jack Chadwick paid for it. Which led more to say Chadwick had been the guilty party to begin with, and Crab Suggs just the scapegoat.

Gay Porter believed that too.

"I guess you can clear, Doris," she said, fiddling with her spoon at her saucer, watching the slender, soft, full-figured girl gather up Senior's dishes. "Doris? Doesn't Turner's sister work for the Chadwicks now?"

"Yes, ma'am. Ginny Lee works there."

"Umm-hmmm, I thought so." She dropped the spoon and began to fold her napkin. "There must be some excitement over at the Chadwicks today."

"Ma'am?"

That was the unknowing look on Doris Towers's face which maddened Gay.

"Delia Benjamin's return," Gay said, and felt like saying, *you know full well!*

"I didn't know Miss Benjamin was back," the colored girl said. She started to leave for the kitchen with the stack of dishes, but Gay said: "You mean to say Ginny Lee didn't mention it down in the Nelly, Doris?"

"She may have, ma'am. I didn't hear it, s'all."

"I suppose it'll *kill* Mrs. Chadwick," Gay said.

Doris stood there holding the dishes, brown-skinned, tall and straight, with the brown eyes that could shine as if she had fever. Gay had seen them once that way, seen her down by the Wheel with Turner, laughing while he was trying to back his car out—but usually Gay saw them the way they were now, solemn, blank.

"I don't know, ma'am," Doris said noncommittally.

"Was she hard to work for?" Mrs. Porter asked her. "I've always heard that Cass Chadwick is a very tempermental type. Never did get over her son's being born blind, that way—like there was some sort of stigma on her. Course a lot of children are born blind and it has nothing whatsoever to do with blood. But I suppose she can't help but wonder sometimes. Beggsom stock was never very high, goodness knows."

Doris Towers said, "I don't know, ma'am."

"Well, law, now, you know whether or not she was a hard person to work for, Doris. Law, I mean—just compare. Would you say she was harder than me to work for, or was I harder than her to work for?"

The girl shifted the arm cradling the plates. "I never had any trouble working for Mrs. Chadwick, ma'am."

"And here?"

"No, ma'am."

"But we're not at all alike, are we, Doris?"

"I don't know, ma'am."

Mrs. Porter sighed. "You certainly are a close-mouthed Nigra girl, aren't you, Doris? Well, all right then, run along to the kitchen. I just thought because you were maid at Chadwicks' once, you might be interested in knowing the news."

The girl said, "Thank you, ma'am," and shoved the swinging door open with her foot.

Gay Porter sat in the crown-backed rosewood chair looking up at the portrait of Cousin Captain Pryce-Bob Tinsel, her hero cousin, who lost a leg at Chickamauga; and beside him, the portrait of Senior's daddy, Calhoun Noailles Porter, blood relative of John C. Calhoun. There was a whole gallery more, all the way around the walls, and all kin with good blood—either on her side or on Senior's. Gay could only wish Troy had appreciated the legacy instead of diluting the blood with Scotch-Irish stock that didn't hold true for more than two generations. But young people don't think a doodely-dong about linage any more, Mrs. Senior Porter thought, rising from the breakfast table, or tradition or genteel living. She crossed the hallway and went into the living room. Young girls would as soon marry some hobo from the state of Washington as a clean-living son of the Cotillion starter. Mrs. Senior Porter always thought of the state of Washington as being occupied entirely by bands of hoboes, when she thought about that state at all, because it was so far off it horrified her to imagine it; and because almost nobody ever knew anyone from there. Crossing the Brussels carpet in the living room—owned by her great-grandmother's Cousin Eugenia and handed down from Mrs. Porter's own mama, with the roses only now getting thin in the pattern—she thought: young men would as soon court some *nouveau riche* trollop born on Tobacco Road who can't tell an antique highboy from a bedroom chiffonier, as court a Key-Ice Belle from Tuscaloosa raised on good manners and Sally Lunn. Thought, standing before the window looking out on Airlie Avenue:

For all the blood in the Benjamins, Dee was a bad apple.

Flo won't make a good Terpsichore; muse of choral singing and dancing ought by rights to be thin, not built like the organ over at the Episcopal Church.

Stood rubbing her arms in the sun of the morning, watching the spider webs glisten on the hedgerows out front by the zinnia bed, thinking: About time! as she watched Poppy pull her roadster up to the curb.

Jud Forsythe was with her, coming up the walk with her now, smoking his old, beat-up pipe, wearing high-tops and a worn-out-in-the-elbows sweater, carrying his old Marine cap, and looking no more like a Minister of the Lord than Tuesday seemed like Sunday.

PART FIVE

"It's nice to see you again," the stranger had said.

He had startled her, coming out from behind the black-gums like that, offering flame for her cigarette. He knew he had—knew by the slight, involuntary jerk to her body as she turned suddenly and faced him; but the slow arch to her eyebrow, and the cool, steady surveillance she gave him with the glistening, jade-shaded, changing green eyes as her lips sucked in the fire and made smoke, belied her surprise; he admired the way she had immediately regained control, and all she had said was:

"Oh?"

"At the drugstore last night. I opened the door for you." He pointed at the cigarette. "You'd just confessed you were a chain smoker."

She had laughed then. She was the sort, he had surmised, who was always sure of herself, always at the reins, imperturbable.

"You have a good memory."

"It's my conceit," he'd answered.

She had on some kind of shirt dress, silken and clinging, with the three buttons that began at the neck, undone; and standing above her he could look down and see that she wore no bra; and see the white swelling flesh of her there, and the nipples awake, and he thought of his lips fastening on to them—gently, he thought, but his good memory haunted him, and like some snag-toothed, lewd and giggling ghost, whispered words once scored in some old text:

> I will drag her, step by step,
> Through infamies unheard of among men;
> She shall stand shelterless in the broad noon
> Of public scorn, for acts blazoned abroad,
> One among which shall be . . . What? Canst thou guess?

He'd turned his eyes away, off to the warm sunshine, sifting through branches of sweet-gum and birch; and as though by some miraculous extrasensory perception she had heard his thoughts, she'd touched her long fingers to the lower button of the three, and looped it shut. And he could feel her action; wondered at the incredible shades of subtleties, unconscious complexities, and hidden human secrets sitting in the middle of the circle of:

"My name is Richard Buddy," he said, looking back at her; at her face, at the dab of red on the tip of her cigarette, sick smoke coming in clouds; and she was beautiful. She shall stand shelterless in the broad noon of public scorn; *why couldn't he stop that from harping on his awareness?*

And, casually—this is the way the circle starts its course—she said, "Hi. I'm Dee," She'd smiled (leading where?). "Dee Benjamin. You're a stranger.

"A visitor."

"Anyone I know?"

But he didn't want to tell her; he wanted to show her. "It's not easy to explain.

"Oh?"

"I'll tell you what," he'd said, "I'm going to speak at noon. Come and hear me. I'd rather explain that way."

"Where?"

"At the courthouse."

She'd jiggled an ash off the tip of the cigarette, cupping her eyes from the sun with her hand as she'd looked up at him. "I can't promise."

"Oh, well, then—" He shrugged.

The same low chuckle—he was conscious of it now, measuring its importance to him—so soon? She wore no rings. "I mean, I don't even know what you're speaking about."

"Come and see then."

"It might not be my cup of tea, Mr. Buddy."

He'd said, "Then again it might."

"I still can't promise."

"I'm not asking you to," he said.

In reflection, as he stood there by the log watching her go up beyond the bown hills, he admired his own agreeable manner; complimented himself on the fact that at no time had he pressed her, neither to come and hear him talk, nor to accept his ride back into Bastrop ("Thanks, but I feel like walking around this morning," she'd said;

*he'd thought: "Why in hell? When we could get to know
one another better?" Thought, Always I feel the pressure
of time; always I am conscious that there is never enough
for me; but merely nodded, "Of course," suavely).*

*In reflection, as he started back across the field toward
the road, he thought, I cannot afford to spend my en-
ergies in an affair. Involvements—those kind—have been
my ruin. I cannot give myself to anything unless I give it
all. Let her go; better she went.*

*Still, when his eyes fell to the sedge of grass under him,
after he picked up the letter which had been dropped
there and read the return address, a smile tipped the
stranger's lips.*

7. *"Everyone is a haunted house. The wise man
knows his ghosts' names. The ignorant man
can't remember."*

         —Jack Chadwick

Benny said, "I didn't marry Maur, Chad. I'm back."
Said it again and again in all the misty early mornings
of yesterday and their long wake-and-turn nights; and today said it: "I'm back. I didn't marry Maur, Chad," just
after Cass left the bed and went into the bathroom, and
Chad fell back for the second sleep, relieved that he no
longer had to feign sleep beside his wife.

Benny walked into the drug store and came back to the
booth where they were sitting and said it; and Chad asked
her: "Benny, will you tell me now? Tell me—*why?* Why
did you leave me?"

And Cass wasn't there any more, only Benny and himself, and the way her fingers touched the nail of his thumb.
"Listen, Chad. Can you hear me? Can you hear me, Chad?
Chad?" coming then from the dream: "Chad, can you
hear me?"

Cassie's voice from the hallway. "Can you hear me,
Chad? Telephone!"

". . . probably nothing serious," he had only half-
listened to Jud Forsythe's voice, cradling the arm of the

phone in his neck, on the pillow, "but I thought you'd want to know."

Half-listening and frustrated by the dreamer's never answered question, sensing the disappointment in the ridiculously real way one does, saying, "Yes, I see," mechanically—"and certainly worth looking into," vaguely; and finally, "Well, thanks, Jud," letting the arm fall back.

Sun flooded the room; and Chad kicked back the pear-shaded summer blanket, saw that it was eight-thirty by the clock; and could hear Johnny-Bob's voice from the bathroom where Cass was probably bathing him. The smell of bacon frying permeated the house, and Chad heard Ginny Lee's voice drift up from the kitchen:

> *"I've got a wife an' a five lit-tle chil-lun*
> *I b'lieve I'll make a trip on the big Mac-Mil-lan,*
> *O Sa-ro Jane, O there's nothin' to do*
> *But set down and sing—"*

He thought of the difference between her and Doris Towers, and he thought of Crabb Suggs knocking Doris down on Love Lucy that night he lied about, and thought (sic!) that Suggs had actually gotten away with it—here in Bastrop—a thing like that happening; and he thought of what Cass had tried to tell him last night in the drugstore; thought, God-Lord, she's probably right; thought of the way this morning when he woke and knew she was, he couldn't just reach and fit her into him and tell her; why? And then thought of what he'd been circling around since he started his walking thoughts: Benny's back.

Remembered the dream, tantalizing: *Benny, will you tell me now? Tell me—why? Why did you leave me?* And as though in this unreal way he could learn the real answer: *Listen, Chad. .*

But all he could hear was her voice telling him that morning in June, years back, over the telephone: "Chad, listen carefully—" While a copy boy behind him was tapping his shoulder, "Mr. Chadwick! Listen, Mr. Chadwick!"

"What, Benny? Can you call me back, honey? I'm in the midst—"

"No, you've got to listen now, Chad. Chad, listen, Maur is here."

"Who?" handing the copy boy a piece of paper and a pencil, saying, "Write it down, for Christ's sake!"

Benny had said, "Maur Granger."

"That's nice. Ask him if he wants to have dinner with us."

"Chad, I've got to tell you something."

The copy boy pushed the paper at him.

"What, Benny? Can I call you right back? Look, I promise . . . ."

"I'm going to marry Maur, Chad. I can't explain it, but I'm going to marry Maur. I'll try and write you a letter. I—" and then the phone's rude click, cutting them off; Chad sitting shock-swollen, his breath stopped, dizzy-headed and incredulous, his eyes looking at the copy boy's message without seeing the words, without caring. The message said: Republic Korea invaded by Reds; and when he tried to call Benny back, Flo Benjamin's sobs said: "G-gone, Jack, my little g-girl," over and over, until the judge's voice interceded.

"You know as much as we do, Jack. They left here about half an hour ago. They must have called you from an outside phone." And then: "Who is he, Jack? This Maur?"

Chad could still vaguely remember that day in front of Jesse Hall, at the University of Missouri. He had been sitting in a group on the steps before the promenade, wait-ing for Benny to come from her 3:30 the way he always did, before they went across to the Shack for some beers with the crowd.

There was someone with her when she came out of Jesse. He was not very tall, just slightly taller than Jack Chadwick himself, and he seemed shy—even from a dis-tance, he was one of those types whose expression and carriage and manner told you instantly that he would be pleasant and polite and eager to please. Chad remem-bered that he was wearing a sports coat and a shirt and tie, with a pair of neatly pressed brown slacks, cut to a taper, and there was a shine to his loafers—he remem-bered because few of the men on campus were so care-fully attired—and at first Jack thought he might be a visitor. He had black hair combed straight and parted well on the side, a short straight nose, soft, curving lips and olive coloring, with handsome dark eyes that seemed never to look directly at another's; dark heavy brows, and good white teeth that flashed in a wide smile when Benny said: "Chad, this is Maury Granger. We have Russian History together."

Benny suggested that the three of them go to Gabe's, a cafeteria, for coffee, instead of joining the crowd at the Shack, because Maury didn't drink; and Maury insisted three times that he could order coke, and refused in a rather not-taking-any-notice way, to relinquish Benny's books to Chad's care.

In Gabe's, Granger was pleasant, directing most of his conversation to Benny, who seemed absorbed by it; but he did not overstay his time, and when he left, Benny only said:

"He's a nice fellow, don't you think, Chad?"

"I suppose," Chad had agreed.

"I think he's sort of—well, wholesome," she had announced.

Shrugging the remark off, Chad had murmured, "Whatever that means."

But Jack Chadwick should have known what that word meant, by Benny's definition; should have remembered how many times Benny had said: "Let's keep our relationship wholesome, Chad. I couldn't bear it if it wasn't. I couldn't marry you."

Because he himself had once said, "You sometimes talk as if the whole idea of sex was unwholesome, Benny. Just because someone says words over your head and you're married doesn't change it from unwholescme to wholesome."

"Then, just let's not let anything threaten our relationship," she had said.

"If you want to be a virgin on the big night, it's okay with me," Chad had answered.

"I don't want anything to happen between us before then," Benny had said solemnly; and so of course, it had— the very next night after she said it, out in a wooded area called the Hinkson, on the outskirts of Columbia, Missouri, under a Harvest Moon, on an Army blanket, at a Hallowe'en Party, after a dozen or more drinks of a concoction called Purple Passion.

Benny had cried afterward, "Oh, my Gawd, Hallowe'en is fatal to me, seems like. I got the curse the first time on Hallowe'en too."

"I'm sorry, Benny," Chad tried.

" . . . didn't want it to happen at all, Gawd—" she cried, with her face in her handkerchief.

"Benny, will you ever forgive me?"

"And you promised you wouldn't spoil our relationship."

"I haven't, Benny. I'm not sorry because it happened between us—"

She wailed, "I am. I didn't come or anything and it was all awful, Chad, and you promised—"

"Benny, listen, I'm not sorry. It didn't spoil anything. Benny, listen, I'm glad it was me the first time. And Benny, listen," holding her in the cold October night, "listen, women don't the first time, see? Women—"

"I did with Jud," she said. "That's why I hated going with him."

Chad was in shock.

She said, "And it was Hallowe'en that time too. It's just spooky!"

"Jesus! Jesus, God, gone-dog," Jack Chadwick said finally, "It sure enough is."

Who is he, Jack? This Maur?

"My confidant," Benny had called him—long after the day out in front of Jesse Hall, after the night on the Hinkson. "I can talk to Maur."

"You can talk to me too, can't you?'"

"Chad, it's different. Remember, I could never talk about Jud and me, to you. Took me ages to confess that."

"I took it all right. Under the circumstances I—"

"But that's just it," she protested. "There aren't any circumstances like that between Maur and me."

Chad said, "Sometimes I wonder."

"You see?" Benny responded. "You're never going to let me forget that thing with Jud. Not really. It's all right that you and Cass Beggsom had a thing, but it's all wrong because Jud and I had a thing. Now you'll accuse me of having things with every man I know."

"Stop calling sex a thing."

"Well, it is a thing! A *thing*, and if you think Maur would let anything happen between us, well, then, you're really dirty-minded, Jack Chadwick, because he's too fine."

"Why don't you marry him, then?" he had snapped.

"Why did you, Benny?"

Chad rolled over on his side and shut his eyes. She had never sent that letter she had promised over the phone, the one explaining. After the click in his ear that morning, Benny had never communicated with him again; and no matter how he strained to remember everything he could about Maur Granger, no matter how earnestly and desperately he searched his memory, he could not find the missing pieces that would fit the puzzle together and provide an answer. After all, she had only met Maur in the last semester of their Senior year; and while they had a few brief, mild arguments over the fact she went to Gabe's with him for coffee a lot, studied Russian History with him out by the Columns, and let him walk her from a class on Red Campus to one on White—and maybe, rarely, went to a movie at the Uptown with him when Chad was cramming, Maur never really seemed to be authentic competition. When Chad and Benny were graduated, after they came back to Basrop, Chad couldn't even remember her mentioning Granger's name—until that day she announced she was going to marry him.

It isn't that I love her any more, God knows, Chad thought, but I wish I knew *why*, wish I knew how I failed her. That's the ghost; not Benny, but the reason Benny left me that way.

"Sleeping, Jack?"

He turned over on his back and looked up at his wife. She was wearing the yellow terry-cloth robe that matched her hair, which was long at her shoulders now, not yet tied back behind her head in the pony-tail; and her face was not made up yet. She had a young, pretty face—Jack used to tease her that she looked just like the movie actress, June Allison—and her expression was tender, and questioning.

He reached out a hand for her and pulled her down on the bed, his face nestling in the crease of her bosom, in an opening in the robe.

"I'm sorry, Cass."

"It's all right," she said. Softly her fingers pressed his temples and moved along the nerve back of his ears, down into his neck.

"That feels good. . . You sure?" he said, "Sure it's all right?"

"I understand. It was a shock. For both of us."

"It's been a bitchy summer all the way around, for you, Cass. I've been pretty hard to live with. I know that. Then last night—well, what I'm trying to tell you, honey is— Listen, Benny doesn't mean anything to me. Do you believe that? She used to, but she doesn't now."

"It's all right, Jack. I understand."

"But I want you to believe me," he said, "and I want you to know you were right about the editorials. It was the wrong tack. I'm not going to run Monday's, Cass."

"All right," she said, "all right, darling . . . What did Jud want this early in the morning?"

"Some screwball gave him a ride this morning," Jack Chadwick said. "Jud says he sounds like he's going to stir up trouble about integration. Says he's from up North, and came all the way down to start trouble in Bastrop."

"Why would anybody bother coming all that distance?"

"There are a lot of nuts loose," Chadwick yawned. "He won't get far. Anyway," he said. "I'm staying out of it." He pulled her back with him on the bed. "How's Mrs. M.?"

"Much better now, thanks," she whispered.

From below Ginny Lee sang:

O there's noth-in' to do
But to set down and sing,
O rock a-bout, my Sa-ro Jane,
Nothin' to do but to set down and sing - - -

The Jack Chadwicks laughed.

"Sometimes I think she believes that," he said.

"Much, much better," she answered. "Darling—"

"I fought and bled in the armed services of the country, but I never got any whiter doin' it."

—Duggan Allen

IT WAS crazy for Duggan Allen to think it but he half did anyway; half thought before the meeting that John Beggsom might maybe lean across the kitchen table and say to Duboe: "Know what, Dube? Riding over here with your nigger this morning, he told me he didn't cotton to Ginny Lee Polk Ann Towers one whit at all. Told me he couldn't be bothered studying any light-skinned housemaid with five names and four eyes. I always thought him and her was sweet on each other, but no, he says; says wouldn't even miss her if she turned to dust next Wednesday and blew away with the wind like a train cinder."

Just to show Duboe what the hell did Duggan Allen care, because Duboe said this morning when he came out to the gin, "Whew! I didn't catch much sleep last night! Some little gals from the Nelly are most practiced, Duggan, hah? A-yeah, what *you* think? You say I was right to make such a statement, or wrong, Duggan, hah?"

Duggan knew Tappie was lying through her front tooth last night when she said, "Naw, course she ain't up, nigger. Ginny Lee Polk Ann ain't gonna study midnight waitin' for yo' black hide to show hisself. She is in on the pallet like any respectable member of Baptist Union Church at this hour."

"Yeah, then what you doin' up, Tappie? If she in sleepin' off Sunday, who you waitin' on, de Lord Jesus?"

"You mind yo' black sassy mouth, nigger! Ginny Lee Polk Ann is where I say."

"Somebody else say she out by the dump a while ago."

"Somebody out by the dump talk dumb talk, and I don't study dumb talkers."

Duggan knew Tappie was lying, knew what Duboe was getting at that morning; now he wished he could get back to Duboe the information that Duggan Allen was a soot-black nigger who didn't think high yeller hung the moon. Let him hump high yeller all he want back in the bushes, cause the good Lord knows that what the bushes is full of, on the first count, is snakes and vipers, like the kind got Eve to begin with.

Duggan drove the pickup down the dirt road away from Beggsom's place, with Beggsom in the front seat beside him. There was going to be a meeting in half an hour, and Duggan was told by Duboe to go and cart Beggsom to it, and Duggan would have liked to know what in hell Beggsom and Suggs and every other gum-assed troublemaker in the county was on their way to being up to.

Still he wished he could get it brought up; maybe just

before the meeting, to show Duboe; and Lawd he guessed he'd kill that five-named four-eyed, milk chocolate bitch by time he caught her that night, once he got off work.

". . . so as I was saying," Duggan told Beggsom, "got me some new tail, lot better 'n her."

"There's nothing wrong with the gin, is there, Duggan?"

"Aw, naw, sir. Don't know what's the meeting for. The boss just said I should go and tote you there."

"Well, I hope he don't need money this time."

"Naw, sir, search me. I don't know . . . Anyway, I don't miss *her*, I tell you."

"Who?"

"Ginny Lee Polk Ann. Lot better'n her."

"Yeah. You boys get a lot of fishing in before you go to grass, I'd guess."

"How much I miss her," Duggan said, "is how much you see the hole if you sticks your finger in a pond and pulls it out and looks for the hole."

"Look down there," Beggsom said. "Down by the Dip."

"Car in trouble."

"Looks like a stranger . . . Yeah, *is*. New York plates."

"Car overheated, heee—lookit! 'Mind me of some women ah know. Now, like Ginny Lee Polk Ann. Used to be I thought she was pretty nice, see. But you know how much I care now for her? It's like when you set out on a cow to catch—"

"He's flagging us down," Beggsom said. "Why'nt you pull over, Duggan? See what it is he wants."

Duggan kept the motor running, and yelled out: "You need help, boss?"

"I stopped to take a leak," the man said; "left my motor running and came back to find it stalled."

"We're going up the road to Chandler's gin," Beggsom said. "Could push you that far, if it'd help."

The man said, "Duboe Chandler?"

"That's right," said Beggsom.

"Look," the man said, "I want to see Duboe myself. How about letting your nigger get my car going, while we ride up together and start him with a push. I'd like to talk with you, if you're a friend of Duboe's."

Beggsom said, "Okay."

Duggan got out. It was crazy for him to have wished it

anyway, wish Beggsom would maybe lean across the kitchen table and say to Duboe: "That nigger of yours—that Duggan, he don't need one gal, he need *ten;* and he got twenty. I used to think he candied to Ginny Lee Polk Ann Towers, but *no,* he says; says wouldn't miss her no more than a duck pond'd miss a hole a finger made in it—" just to show Duboe what the hell did Duggan care. But then, as Duggan got into the Chevy and watched through the rear mirror for the pickup to come up from behind, his eye caught a stack of pamphlets. Whatever the hell the words said he'd never know, but the picture on the front said something that would show Ginny Lee Polk Ann just how much Bible-swearing *he'd* do by Tappie's word; just exactly how much he knew about white vipers in the bushes with colored Eves; just spelling-out-in-the-sky-with-an-airplane what he knew she'd been up to.

Duggan reached a long arm back and took one of the pamphlets off the pile.

Then he felt the pickup bump him forward.

9.   *"What's it doing out?"*

—Mrs. Gus

THE ONLY TWO who didn't call her Mrs. Gus were Gus Chandler and Duboe, her son; and except for Duggan Allen, who did her errands when they could spare him from the gin, they were the only two who really saw her. Sometimes, like this morning, she would crawl out of the big iron bed which was heaped with magazines, scratch paper and stubby pencils, and go and stand by the crack in the doorway of her room, next to the kitchen; and sometimes, one of the men sitting around the table there—drinking coffee and gabbing, like now; or playing poker and beer drinking, like other times, would be aware of the shadow, or the faint pink color of her wrapper, and know she was up and prying, but beyond that they didn't care to see or think. She was Gus and Duboe's problem.

Beggsom was the exception, but even old John never saw her. He thought to bring her magazines, though; old issues left behind in one of the cabins out in back of his place, where he still got an occasional tourist. He'd tie a string around a stack of them and he'd do what he did this morning—just hand them to Gus, and end the matter right there. Gus never actually thanked him, merely reached out his red wrists and grabbed them with his work-rough hands, nodded or mumbled, "All right, I got 'em." No one ever figured out what got Beggsom started doing it, or *why* he did, maybe because no one thought very hard on the subject.

In Bastrop proper, there was the rumor she was crazy, but out at Gus's she was just a fact everyone accepted. She was Mrs. Gus and she stayed in her room, and people who lived out there or came and went out there with any regularity, had long ago stopped commenting on the fact.

Gus himself never mentioned her, but occasionally, when he went in there for some reason, he could be heard calling her "little girl Lettie" or "Lettie-Lou," always in the tenderest tones, and Duboe never refrained from mentioning her, but spoke of "Mommie," said things like: "I was telling Mommie this morning—" "When I took the papers to Mommie—" or: "Have to get Mommie's radio fixed down at town,"—in a random, off-hand way, as though any boy's mommie might one day decide to haul all her belongings down to a windowless room that had once served as a pantry, and stay in there for five years.

By actual count it was five years, four months, and nineteen days. Lettie-Lou had checked it only a few hours before the men came. It was important to know, because this time she had a plan she was convinced would work; this time she was sure it would not be long before she could announce to Gus and Dubby: "I been asked."

Duggan was already near to carrying out her instructions, and Mrs. Gus walked barefoot around the wooden floor, pulling out the folds of her wrapper and giggling softly to the walls.

On the bed, piled high with copies of *Your Life, House Beautiful,* and *Seventeen,* was the new magazine which Mrs. Gus had never seen: *Charming,* open to the article she had finished reading last night: CHARMING YOUR WAY INTO THOSE VERY SPECIAL GROUPS . . . .

She had liked that article better than CHARMING YOUR HUSBAND'S BOSS (Gus was his own boss!), CHARMING

AFTER FIVE, CHARMING AT A CHILI BUFFET, OR CHARMING IN
THE "POURING-DOWN."

With a new glimmer to her tired light-blue eyes, she
had sat on the bed under the naked electric bulb which
hung from a black cord above her, squeezing her long toes
in delight as she read:

"*You know who we mean . . . the very special . . .
special in everything they do—They have a flair—a way—
a secret something about them that makes you say: 'Me
too?' 'Can I play?' Oh, maybe it's the scrumptious center-
piece on their buffet table (just a feather and some multi-
colored thimbles, but you try to do it and you're all
thumbs) or maybe it's that extra little red ribbon under the
pearl lapel pin—but—*"

On and on she had read, shaking her gray head up and
down vigorously, and when she came to the five-point
program she copied down each point in her neat, curly
hand, in ink on lined paper, the way she kept all important
notations.

Studying the list long past midnight—she had even heard
Dubby come in, called out to him: "Dubby, what's it doing
out?" and he'd called back, "Stopped raining, Mommie.
G'night."—still, stayed there in the bed with her light
burning, going over the list and trying to decide which one
was *the* one.

Some of them just weren't right—number 4, for instance.
If she were to get it told around that she and Gus were
giving a cruise party, Flo Benjamin would call it a lie, like
Gay Porter and the rest would; would cackle: "A cruise
party out to the Chandlers'. Haw-w-hee, gaw, that's a lulu!"

And Number 3 didn't make good sense. If she were to
go around Bastrop carrying a gaily colored umbrella, even
when it wasn't raining, like the magazine said, everyone
would sure say she was off her stick.

She'd studied the list and studied it, and then it struck
her—Number 5! Her heart raced and pounded and she
had to laugh, law, Number 5! If anything would do it, that
one would: SPLURGE ON SOME EXPENSIVE, FRAGRANT SOAP
FOR YOUR GUEST BATHROOM.

It took her two more hours to page through the magazine for the name of a soap, and to write out the message
on the violet note paper, and after that was over, she

couldn't sleep. She kept tossing and turning and thinking of morning, when Duggan came and she sent him off on the errand.

She hadn't counted on the meeting Gus had called.

"Now, Lettie-Lou," he said. "Duggan'll do your errand when he brings John down from his place. There's plenty of time for your errand, honey."

"You know how long it's been now, Gus?"

"Yeah, Lord, Lettie, little girl, now, you g'wan back to bed, now, that's a big girl."

"And this time they won't disappoint me, Gus. Not no more. Flo Benjamin never did have my hand. I beat her in penmanship, you know, Gus. Did I tell you I beat her? It was a county-wide contest, that summer of the Galveston hurricane. She shouldn't be putting on airs, when I'm the one who won. Took first place and she was only honorable mention, Gus. I swear it on a stack of Bibles. It's the truth!"

"All right, now, Lettie-Lou. All right now."

"You'll be seeing, Gus. Maybe by nightfall."

That morning as she stood in the crack of the door listening, before Duggan brought Beggsom there, she could hardly concentrate on what the men were saying. Sometimes, so she could remember the conversations, she wrote them down in notebooks with a pencil, and read them over at night and thought about them, but whenever she had a *new plan,* it took all her energy. Like today.

She heard Crabb Suggs say: "Hell, Duboe's got something more than just a gripe for us to get out of our systems, with this nigger thing. Hell, since that goddam black ape started his own store down near the feed company, the jigaboos buy from him. Niggers buy from niggers, when they can, and I'm tired of these school-learned niggers that get it in their wool heads they're too good for the gins and the fields any more. My store's going out of business, goddam it!"

Mrs. Gus wrote: "store going out of b." but then looked behind her on the cluttered bureau and saw the violet envelope; and bit on the rubber eraser of the pencil, smiling. Gay Porter would probably call up Flo Benjamin right away.

". . . like to break his neck for him," Duboe Chandler

was saying, "when he ran them articles on the croppers' diet, 'member?"

"Yeah, *do* I!" Gus Chandler slapped the table with his large hand. "Hell. I had croppers on my land b'fore that bastard was standing up to pee, 'n he gonna tell *me* some nigger dream like pellagra caused by fatback and pot likker!"

Suggs laughed, "P'lagra caused by every darn thing the nigger *gets,* caused by; caused by the fact he got no buttons on his pants."

Duboe said, "John don't cotton to him even though Cass hooked up with him."

"We gonna get the niggers," Chandler said, "or Jack Chadwick?"

"Git what there is to git," said Suggs. "Nobody looks like a black ape is goin' to school with my boy or my girl. You sold me, Duboe."

Mrs. Gus always omitted the dirty words when she took down the conversations. Men could rarely help it, particularily men from the land. "They just talk that way, goddam it, Lettie-Lou!" her daddy used to say when she was a child, and Gus courting her, "and sure, maybe they can't strut Miss Lucy Hill as fine as them white knuckles you go to high with, but a man who works on the land is a man, baby. And only a man can make you feel like a woman!"

Mrs. Gus wandered around her room touching her finger to dust screens and thinking back to when she won the penmanship prize. The year of the Galveston hurricanes, and Flo Fulton Benjamin got only honorable mention; and Mrs. Gus's daddy cried, first time and only time—right there in the auditorium.

Before she quit going to church down at Second Methodist she told Reverand Baird once about it, and he said: "Why, Mrs. Gus, I think you should be mighty proud."

But Gus and Duboe just kept grabbing napkins and soaking up the creamed chicken she'd spilled all over the table; and there were people around her snickering, and Lettie-Lou never knew why, so she wouldn't go back.

Dubby said they were all skunks down at that church.

Mrs.Gus giggled. She'd go back, one day; maybe even one day this week; and she skipped across to the sink, lit a match and looked up at the calendar. It was Saturday, all right. Maybe tomorrow.

The door of the porch opened then.

Mrs. Gus ran to the crack in her own doorway. There was a stranger, a tall, young stranger, standing by the kitchen table with John Beggsom.

". . . fellow I was telling you about. Hell," Duboe said grinning, "this is a coincidence."

"Met him on the road," Beggsom said.

Beggsom pulled out a chair, and pointed to one for the stranger. "What's this all about, now?" he asked.

"It's about niggers," Duboe answered.

Gus Chandler said, "Here comes Duggan. Stall off a second."

Mrs. Gus heard her husband's steps start toward her room.

She grabbed the envelope and held it behind her back, but she couldn't keep the grin from curling her lips. He closed the door behind him.

"Have you got something for Duggan to do, little girl?"

"Yes. An errand."

"To the drugstore, Lettie-Lou?"

Mrs. Gus hesitated.

"Lettie-Lou, lookit, honey," Gus said. "I pay that boy to gin cotton. Now, it's in season, and I can't spare him. And I can't spare a picker, either. Not just to go down to the drugstore and tell lies, Lettie-Lou. Now, they know we ain't inherited no money, or we ain't come across no famous ancestor, or we ain't got a reward or an *a-ward* of any kind. Now, little girl, there's no sense sending Duggan there to sit on a stool and lie. People ain't even going to listen."

Mrs. Gus smiled. "You know how long it's been now, Gus?"

"Yeah, Lettie, and I know you won the penmanship contest, and I know you never meant to throw the creamed chicken, down to church, but—"

"Oh, I never threw it, Gus."

"What do you want him to say?" Gus sighed. "What's Duggan supposed to say this time?"

"It's a note, this time," Mrs. Gus said, "a note requesting a special kind of soap."

He held his hand out. "Let me see it, Lettie-Lou."

"You won't rip it up?"

"No."

"Gus, you *swear?*"

"Swear!" he answered solemnly.

She handed it to him, and he took it out of the envelope. He jerked the electric light chain; then, mumbled as he read:

Please rush by this boy six pieces of expensive, fragrant soap:

Savon
a l'eau de cologne
Jean Marie Farina
Roger & Gallet
successeurs
maison fondee a Paris en 1806
New York   Paris.
We are splurging for guests who are very special.
Lettina Louise Chambers Chandler

He looked across at her.

"What the hell is this, Lettie-Lou? This is what? Mumbo-jumbo?"

"I copied the soap right out of here." She started for the magazine, but he stopped her, placing his hands on her shoulders. She was a small, very thin woman, pale and frowning. There were no more buttons on the front of the wrapper and she held it tightly around her.

"You want this soap?" he said. "You really want this?"

"Gus, it's just a little plan. It won't hurt nothing."

"You want the soap, Lettie?"

"Oh, yes. I want it. I do, Gus."

"They ain't gonna believe nothing about no guests, Lettie."

"I read up, Gus."

"You can stay in here and read up and read up," her husband said, "but there ain't gonna be no invitation forthcoming from those Methodist Amuses. God damn it, Lettie, how'd you ever go off your head because of them? How'd you ever—"

She was looking at him with tears close to coming in her eyes.

"You think there's something funny about me, don't you, Gus?"

He sighed, "Naw, Lettie. Naw, I didn't mean that."

"I was just as pretty as they were, Gus. Senior Porter asked me to drive with him once. I remember, it was the summer—"

"Give me the letter, Lettie," Gus Chandler said. "I'll get Duggan to take it down."

"It's close to noon now, Gus. Senior will be home for lunch. I'd like for Senior to handle my account, so Duggan better go right on to the Porters. Then tell him to come and bring me the soap and tell me the answer they sent." She giggled. "Will you, Gus?"

"Yes, Lettie," he said. "I will."

He started toward the door.

Mrs. Gus said, "Gus?"

"Huh?"

"Gus, tonight maybe—tonight maybe I can say I been asked."

10. *When I was a kid, some white men down at the feed company where I worked told this joke: A Negro fell off a ten-story building. On his way down, his buddy yelled, "Stop, Rastus, you'll kill yourself!" Rastus yelled back, "I can't stop!" His buddy yelled again. "Stop, Rastus, you'll land on top a white woman." Before you knew it, Rastus shot back up on top the building . . . I remember how everyone laughed. But I just sat there thinking, Gawd, what if he'd landed on her! And I used to dream, when I was a kid, that I was Rastus, trying to stop myself in mid-air from falling on a white woman.*

—Turner·Towers

HE USED to wake up in a sweat from that dream, a cold sweat that left him shivering on his pallet, and whimpering until Tappie, his grandmaw, who some said never slept, closed her eyes but was always awake her whole life, crawled across to him and took his skinny boy's body into her own thin and bony frame, and said: "Hush up, nigger boy. You wake your daddy up, he go'n tan your brown hide till the blood flow like water outa de white folks taps."

He used to tell her about the dream and she used to tell him back, "Next time someone yell dat to you when you's dreaming, yo' say back in de dream dat you know for a fact it ain't no white woman you's fallin on, it's a white cushion, big as a wagonfull of cotton and just as soft. And you go right on falling, boy, but don't be wakin' up and cryin' out when yo' daddy got to be up at quarter to six."

Turner used to think about the dream over the years. and remember the fear; and he used to marvel at the fact that as a kid he'd feared hurting a white woman more than smashing his bones on concrete; and that as a man, flying with the 332nd Fighter Group, after the attack on the bloody Anzio beachhead, when he managed to extricate himself from his wildly diving plane, and get his parachute open, he thought the crazy ironical thought: *Stop, Rastus,* floating down the three thousand feet in the gray overcaast, dizzily bobbing with his feet dangling, *"You'll land on top a white woman."*

That Saturday morning, hurrying from his store down on Rex Road behind the Bastrop Feed Company, on his way to Porters', the dream came to his mind once more, after a long hiatus during which he had managed to save, and to swing a bank loan, to set himself up in the grocery business, and to realize a certain satisfaction in his means for livelihood; one he never knew before. And now the first threat to that security—what Doris had told him over the telephone—and along with it, the dream, re-remembered.

In Bastrop they say the Negroes smell smoke first; say white folks can tell trouble coming by the Negroes going; that it seeps into white folks' awareness in the same slow way air seeps out of a tire; that the Negroes are going straight to the Nelly after work, and that the door those nights in the Nelly are shut to the outside, and the inside is dark. Watch out if Negroes don't loiter during a noon hour down by the Wheel, the whites say; and wonder, when the Negroes don't make town of a Saturday, in slow, ambling, easy-laughing groups. The Negroes are quicker when the air is ominous, and they are quieter. And some say their eyes move differently when they know a danger; say a Negro can't keep his eyes averted from a white's then, but in one, fast, and impulsive glance up, meets the white

man's look head-on, for one split second of his black eterni-
ty, and that is the siren, his eyes seeing yours, some say—
that is the whistle screaming *caution.*

But sometimes long before all of this, some more subtle
sign may show itself, and a white hand may pause at work
to scratch the white head and wander, like Jack Chadwick
—watching Turner Towers from the window of the
Citizen:

"How come Turner's taking off work right at noon hour
when he's busiest?"

Then shrug and forget.

And less curiously, more politely, another in the town
may notice—Senior Porter—on his way to his car out in
front of Porter Drugs: "Well, now, Turner, how come
you're taking off, hah? Must be you're a boy doing yourself
ho-kay, hah?"

"As a matter of fact, sir, I'm on my way to your place.
Have to see my wife for a bit."

"Good enough. Come on, drive along with me."

Turner could wonder at his own vulnerability to the least
sign of trouble; could and did feel the familiar irritations
mount in him now as he got into the black Plymouth on
Court Street; thought, and knew as he thought, that he
was thinking like a Negro now—the first admission to himself he saw the smoke signs clearly marked, decimating the
man, personalizing Color, making stripes in the front seat,
black and white:

Thought: You're a boy doing yourself ho-kay; naw, I'm
a man, Mr. Porter, black as your counter top and grub-
bing for my collard greens, and my wife scrapes your
dishes and burns your trash, and we live in the Nelly with
the rest of the niggers; got our B. A.'s from Talladega
tacked up in our outhouse.

Thought: passing the Wheel on the way up Franklin,
"I know your boy well, Mr. Porter; met him in Cannes
at a rest resort for soldiers. A French boy went to the
trouble of bringing us together 'cause he knew we were from
the same home town; surprised us, Mr. Porter, out on the
porch, Troy in a wheelchair there. French boy said, "You
two didn't even know you were in the same hospital! I
knew you'd be surprised to see each other! I'll leave you
alone," the French boy said, "you'll have a lot to talk
about . . .". I guess we talked and laughed for hours, Mr.

Porter, Troy and me. We couldn't get enough said about Bastrop . . . And after the war I saw him in your place, one night, saw him with Miss Poppy, as he introduced her. He said, "Miss Poppy, this is the colored boy I was telling you about—that I met in Cannes. Name's Turner," he said. Said if I ever wanted an odd job for some extra money, I should look him up; they had a boy to cut the lawn, but he made a mess of hedges. Said was I good at hedges?

Thought: passing the Episcopal Church on Allen, Senior Porter humming along with the radio: Tired of having no last name, and only one age—boyhood—nigger never gets to be a man; and thought: got to get a grip; maybe not as bad as it sounds; maybe everything going to be ho-kay, like Mr. Porter say; Lord, pray, Lord.

"Well, here we are, boy," Senior Porter said as they swung into the gravel drive. "Whoop, there's Duggan on the steps. Must be another crazy message from Mrs. Gus."

"Yes, sir," Turner said, getting out of the car on his side.

Senior Porter walked around to the front of the house and Turner went over to Duggan.

"Let's see it," he said.

"Now, you listen, Turner, 'fore you git mad. I was only gonna tease Ginny Lee Polk Ann. You know I soft on dat sister yours. I wasn't meaning anythin' at all, Turner."

"Duggan, this hasn't got anything to do with you and Ginny. I just want to see that pamphlet and hear where you got it."

Duggan bit into an apple he was holding; talked with his mouth full, chewing: "Got it from a man we picked up by the Dip. Had car trouble. I had to git in his car to git it started, and I sees the pamphlet, s'all. So I says, maybe like I'll play a joke on—"

Turner held his arm down so Duggan could take another bite.

"Where is it?" he said.

"Doris snatched it from me. Saw it hanging outa my pocket when I come to bring de note from Mrs. Gus. She got it."

Turner went up the steps and through the screen door. His wife stood by the stove.

"On the table," she said. "Looks like Council or Ku Klux."

"Because of Monday." Turner said matter-of-factly, walking over to the dinette.

"Under the toaster, Turner. God, I hope it doesn't start up."

"And Duggan said there was a meeting out there?"

"Suggs, Beggsom, the Chandlers—all of them, and this man in the car."

Turner studied the front:

Could this be
YOUR FAIR LADY
in the near future?

"Don't know the man's name or anything about him?" Turner asked, leafing through the pamphlet.

"Duggan said he was from up North."

Turner Towers frowned. "From up North? That don't make sense!"

"There's something else," his wife said, "something I didn't tell you, Turner, This morning," she began, "Reverend Forsythe stopped by with Miss Poppy. He called Mr. Jack about a man who'd picked him up—same place, out by the Dip—and he said—"

They were interrupted by a sudden burst from the dining room, Gay Porter laughing: "Hoooooo, gaw, law-gaw, Senior, Lettie-Lou Chandler is plumb cuckoo! Now, you just listen here to what this says—"

"Go on!" both men said to their wives.

11.   *"Then everything went haywire—all of a sudden, on a Saturday . . ."*
—Poppy Porter

WHERE we going, Mom?" the small boy asked. "Don't stand on the seat when I'm driving, Pryce!" she snapped. "I've told you that time and time again and you don't pay any attention!"

"But where we going?" he slid down and sat sulking beside his twin, May B., who was turning the pages of a Golden Story Book.

May B. whined: "Pryce always stands up."

"Both of you be quiet!" Poppy Porter told them. "I don't know where we're going," she said, but she had known since the roadster passed the Wheel on Court Street that she was going to see Jack Chadwick.

She insisted to herself that she did not have to analyze her reasons for taking such a step, and yet at the same time she analyzed one possible reason out of existence. Her visit had nothing to do with Dee's return. She had no curiosity to see for herself how Chad was taking it. This, she told herself, was the farthest thing from her mind that Saturday afternoon. And so was anything and everything that had happened between Jack and herself.

Still, a gap of five years had never actually been bridged. It had remained by mutual consent—as tacitly understood as it was understood not to refer to the past, not *that time* in the past, anyway, when Poppy was chasing Chad. There was no doubt in anyone's mind—not even in Poppy's —that "chasing" was the only word to describe it.

It irritated Poppy, to this day, whenever she and Troy were out on a party, or over at the Yellowhammer, or down in Porter Drugs, that Troy would place his hand on her somewhere—perhaps press her thigh, under the table, or touch a finger to her wrist, or move his palm gently against her back—as a signal that Chad and Cass were on their way to join them momentarily, to chat briefly for a time. It was a signal, Poppy knew, and it was intended as a tender gesture of sympathy, she supposed, perhaps completely unconscious on Troy's part; still she never failed to flinch inwardly when it happened. It seemed to her preposterous for Troy to want to remind her, or offer her solace after all those years. And equally preposterous, that between Chad and herself there existed some sort of desperate politeness, a screen of solicitous discretion, as though each one were forever skirting an issue as embarrassing as a recent death, hereditary insanity, or hemorrhoids.

In the back seat, as the roadster turned down West Tennessee, the twins were fighting over the Golden Story Book, and Poppy could feel impatience well up in her. She tried to temper it with the thought that they were too young to know what was happening, but when Pryce thrust a hand holding a silver pistol over the seat, and said: "Tell me why we're stopping here, or I'll blast you!"

she literally shrieked: "Because we *have* to stop here, Pryce!"

And that much was true, she decided. It was not, as it may have seemed, such a random decision to go to Chad, though she knew as well as she knew her husband, that Troy, when he heard about it, would say, "I wish you'd think things through, and not always act on impulse."

Cutting the motor, she felt in her bag for a dime to put in the meter. "I want you and May B. to wait in the car," she said. "And I want you to behave. Please." Through the rear-view mirror she saw Pryce slouched in the corner, frowning, his fingers pulling at his lip, the same hurt expression covering his countenance that showed on Troy's face whenever he was offended.

Like last night, driving home from the Yellowhammer, after she had remarked: "It was Dee who hurt Chad, Troy," when they were discussing Dee's return, "not the other way around. Chad wouldn't hurt anyone intentionally."

Sulking, he had said, "He didn't hurt you?"

"I hurt myself," she had lied. "Chad never let me think for a minute that he'd marry me—or that he even cared for me, for that matter."

Somehow it always gave her more satisfaction to pretend that Chad hadn't led her on. It made her seem more noble to have loved a man who would not purposely deceive her, for even though love exists primarily in the eye of the beholder, as beauty does, the beholder rarely wants to admit myopia. Confirmation of the prize helps, and since there was no one in Bastrop to confirm that Poppy had a prize in Jack Chadwick—for everyone knew he saw her only in the blinding light of the torch he carried for Dee— Poppy herself had to lie before others, to save her self-respect.

And every time she did it, Troy sulked, because it was such an obvious lie.

"I want to go back and see the circus at the Wheel," May B. spoke up.

Pryce said, "So do I."

"It isn't a circus," Poppy told them, getting out of the roadster ."Now, you all behave, hear?"

"What is it, then?" Pryce said. "There's a whole crowd."

"There's a whole crowd," May B. echoed him. "There's a whole crowd."

Poppy said. "It's a gathering. Just some people who are going to listen to a speech."

"I want to go and shoot them!" Pryce cried out.

Poppy said, "So do I, Pryce."

"Then, let's!" he waved the silver pistol triumphantly.

"Put it away," Poppy told him. "Now, I won't be long. You all behave."

May B. said, "Pryce always stand up on the seat, doesn't he, Mommie. Just like a coward!"

Dropping the dime in the meter, Poppy tried to think where her daughter heard that word. Then she remembered: Yesterday afternoon the twins were playing on the porch when Troy was discussing his opponent with the men up from Montgomery.

"Polk just pussy-foots around the whole issue of integration," Troy had said. "Lord, you'd think he was running for the United States Senate, 'stead of the State of Alabama's. Well, I got him there. He's a coward, s'all."

"What're you going to say?" one of the men had said, mopping his brow in the heat and chewing on the soggy end of the smoked-down cigar, "That's still a big issue, Troy."

"Not for a State Senator. Hell, I'm going to say just what the Alabama' motto says: We Dare Defend Our Rights."

"Good point!" the man said, "just quote the motto. Sure that's the motto?"

Poppy glanced at her reflection in the plate glass window of the Fair-Deal Furniture Store, next to the *Citizen*. She wished she didn't look quite so tacky; wished she'd known when she left the house this morning to pick up the twins at her in-laws', that she was going to call on Chad— but that was like someone wishing they had thought to bring an umbrella on one of those utterly sunny summer days, when a sudden unexpected downpour caught them unaware. She would have liked to be wearing a dress; but she was wearing her years-old dirndl skirt, and the mended nylon blouse; and she would have liked to be wearing heels, but in her effort to try and be punctual—Gay Porter had some kind of fetish about people being on time—she had slipped her feet into a pair of scuffed loafers.

Plain tacky, she thought, as her hand touched the doorknob of the *Citizen's* office, and for the first time since she had made the decision to come here, she regretted it. She thought of going home and changing first, or of calling Chad from home, even though the way she looked shouldn't have anything to do with what she was seeing him about.

Then Chad's voice voided any impulse she had to turn back.

"Poppy!" he was smilinag, standing in the hallway outside his office. "Nice to see you."

She saw his hand shut the door behind him, and she said, "I came to see you about something important, Chad."

"I saw you pull up," he answered.

They stood there some slow seconds, facing one another —she waiting for him to ask her into the office, and Chad waiting for her to continue.

Finally, Chad said, "We're in a rush. Office is all messed up, Poppy."

"I won't take much of your time."

"Good!" he said so emphatically that Poppy Porter looked up into his eyes; and he turned them from her and glanced over at the wall where there was a bulletin board, with farm prices pasted to it. He said, "I don't mean that I wouldn't spare you all the time you needed, Poppy, any day but today. I—right now—I got to take care of something. Something come up."

She felt better then. Perhaps he already knew. "You know what's going on down at the Wheel, Chad?"

"Is something going on down there?"

"There's a stranger in town—"

He interrupted her. "Yeah, Jud called me from Senior's. Some crackpot." His tone was curt, restless.

"It's more serious than that," she said. She saw his fumbling impatience with her; saw it and couldn't help remembering when he used to complain: "God almighty, Poppy, you take so damn long to say anything! Can't you talk any faster than you do!" That recollection confused her all the more, and triggered a whole series of memories that she kept forcing off her mind's screen, as she stood there in the hallway, wishing to God she hadn't come here; beginning to realize for the first time that she was nothing but a source of angry embarrassment to Jack Chadwick; that traces of the same widely unreasonable agitation which he had shown with her toward the end of their affair, were evident now. Poppy could feel the heat rise in her cheeks, and she knew her face was that ugly red color that came whenever she felt humiliated.

"Well, what *is* it, Poppy!" He let his annoyance show clearly for the first time; then sighed, "God, I don't mean to be short with you, Poppy, but things are in a state."

Poppy let the words rattle out of her like keys clicking out exercises on a typewriter machine: "This stranger is stirring up trouble, Chad. I came to you because Troy is down in Montgomery and I didn't know who else to come to. Right now at the Wheel there's a crowd and he's down there, this stranger that Jud picked up on the road, down there talking against integration. I passed him in the car on my way here. There's a lot of people, Chad, people from all around Tate County, it seems, and he's down there—"

Again, Jack Chadwick interrupted her. "Poppy, why did you come to me?"

She looked at him incredulously. "W-what?" For one split second she lost all track of the reason she *had* come; couldn't remember that she had come because Chad seemed the only logical person in Bastrop to tell, because she *knew* Jack's stand on integration, because she had spent a summer defending his editorials before Troy and her father; couldn't remember any of that, but could just stand there looking at him, close to crying, the way it used to be whenever Jack reprimanded her over the slightest little thing she'd said or done.

He said, "I'm not the law, Poppy."

"I know that," she answered; thinking what made me think I could bridge that gap, walk from then to now without falling on my face? Thinking: I'd forgotten what it was like—the then. Forgotten the way Chad could look at me like I was dirt.

"Poppy, look, I'll look into it, all right? I'll take a walk over there later and see about it, okay?" His hand behind him groped for the doorknob to his office.

She said, "I just came from Dad's," reaching trancelike into her bag for the piece of crumpled paper. "This was in their milk bottle this morning." She held it out to him.

Jack took it, and frowning, tearing the paper in his hurry to open it, said, "Let's see here—"

But the tears in Poppy's eyes were too close to spilling over, the hurt and shame too urgent for her to contain much longer.

She said, "Maybe it's nothing, Chad. I have to run anyway. The twins are in the car out front."

As she turned and started out the door, she heard Chad answer: "I'll look into it, Poppy. I promise, gal," and his voice had that high, nearly giddy tone, of sudden, welcome relief.

PART SIX

"*. . . and now I'm going to mention the name of Noah!*"
the stranger said, under the ginkgo, down at the Wheel,
"and I'm going to tell you something about myself. I'm
only a man; I'm no more than a man, I'm no less than a
man. I've done things that were wonderful, and things that
were mediocre; things that were sinful, and things that
were foolish. I'm not a saint and I don't know any saints.
But, I'll tell you something—I don't like atheists. I don't
feel comfortable around atheists. Okay, maybe they're bril-
liant, some of them, maybe they know all about this Sig-
mund Freud, and this nuclear fission, and this theory of
evolution—but I'm going to tell you something else. I don't
feel at home with people who try to tell me that the way
I court a girl has got something to do with the way I sat
on the toilet when I was five years old; and—don't laugh,
because the Freud clan will tell you a lot of things sicker
than that—and, I don't feel at home with people who
tinker with foul-colored liquids in test tubes, and come up
with split atoms; and I'll tell you something else—I don't
care what the schoolbooks say, or what the eggheads say, or
what those bespectacled, bow-tied bowlegged, absent-
minded Harvard professors say, I don't feel at home with
people who say my ancestors hung from trees! I just don't!"

The stranger paused for the spontaneous applause, un-
smiling, head up, eyes turned toward the flag on top of the
pole across the street on the courthouse lawn; then raised
his palm and looked to his audience.

He said, "Thank you."

He stuck one hand in the pocket of his gray flannel trou-
sers, and shifted his weight from one leg to the other,
straight-standing and tall, and in his deep, sure tone, con-
tinued: "I feel at home with folks who like God. I've al-
ways known that kind. I feel at home with folks who fear
God. I've always been that kind.

"Now," he said, "I'm going to talk about Noah. Noah
had three sons, and one of them was called Ham. Whether

or not you people know it, Ham is the reason I came all the way down here to see you. It's in the Bible—the story of what Ham did, and I suppose you all remember it. Remember, one day. Noah was taking a nap—a hot day, like today. Now, how many of us on a blistering hot day have been known to go on into the bedroom, and peel our clothes off, and take a nice nap? Well, that's what Noah was doing when Ham walked in his room. Walked in and saw his father there and stood there and looked at his father's nakedness. And then, ran off giggling and laughing and telling dirty stories about what he'd seen to his brothers. His brothers, mind you, respected their father, and they went in and covered him up."

The stranger sighed. "I don't blame Noah for being mad. I don't blame him for being disappointed. And I don't blame him for deciding that Ham just wasn't up to bearing the responsibility of an independent man of integrity and good moral nature."

"So—" the stranger took his hand out of his pocket and rested it on his hip— "Noah said, 'Ham, you—and all your sons, all those who come after you and are your blood, are to be servants.' To quote Noah's exact words 'Cursed be Ham; a servant of servants shall he be unto his brethren!'"

The stranger lowered his hand to his side. "Ham is the Egyptian word for "black," ladies and gentleman. Ham was a Nigra, ladies and gentleman, the first Nigra on this earth—and his own father knew him for what he was! His own father knew Ham was always going to be giggling and telling dirty stories and peeking around trying to see nakedness—unless someone took him under his wing and put him to work and saw to it he behaved. His own father knew he wasn't fit to be anything but a servant! His own—"

A husky voice from the audience yelled: "How come Noah had a nigger for a son!"

The stranger paused a moment, straightened his thin, navy-blue tie; then said in a calm voice: "I'm glad you asked me that. I meant to mention it. You see, in the beginning, folks, God was just as willing to give the Nigra an equal footing. God made one of Noah's sons black for that reason, to see if the Nigra wasn't just as healthy, and moral, and responsible as the white man. Never mind what the atheists tell you, and never mind what the eggheads tell you, and never mind what the Supreme Court tells you, ladies and gentlemen. God put the Nigra to test way back when the earth was created, and the Nigra just wasn't up to par! God decided then and there that the Nigra should be a servant! God, ladies and gentlemen, gave his views on integration right in the Bible, Genesis Nine, Verse Twenty-five. Go home tonight and read it, and then sit down and ask your heart—search your heart—and ask yourself if what is about to happen right here in Bastrop on Monday morning is what God would have wanted!"

The Wheel exploded with hoots and hooray's and hand-aching applause.

The stranger still did not smile.

12.   *"I'm back, Chad."*
          —A voice in a dream

HE SHUT the door of his office behind him. "I hated to treat Poppy like that."

Delia Benjamin sat in the wooden chair beside his desk, the ashtray at her elbow filled with stubbed-out cigarettes, their tips red with her lipstick.

She said, "I'm sorry. Maybe I shouldn't have come here."

"I'm glad you came, Benny," he said. He walked over to the window, his black copy pencil still stuck behind his ear, the green plastic eye-shade pushed back on his brush-cut, rust-colored hair; and he thought how inadequate words were, how they deceived and said nothing so often; and how well they camouflaged thoughts. For when she walked in that door some fifteen minutes ago, and when Jack Chadwick looked up and saw her face, his stomach had turned over, and his brain had stopped any thinking, and instantly he had had a sensation of fear, diluted with joy. It was strange that all the times in the past when he had tried to imagine this moment, it had never occurred to him that fear would have a part in it. He had sat at his desk worrying whether his hands would be steady enough to light her cigarette, and thinking simply how incredibly beautiful she was, marveling that he could have forgotten that about Benny. For it was equally strange that all the times in the past, when he had remembered her, he had remembered something they had done together, something she had said, or some way about her—the almost naive way she talked about her fear of death, the way she lit one cigarette from another, or the way she peeled off her nail polish from her fingers, leaving little red specks in her lap. He hadn't ever actually remembered the features of her face, or her figure; never actually framed her in his memory as a woman he saw with his eyes, the way he saw her that Saturday afternoon.

She had come to him about a letter she had lost while she was taking a walk that morning out at the Dip. There was no one else, she said, to whom she could go. It was a letter which she had written to Maur, and the contents were not very pleasant. Was there any way he could think of for her to find it? She had searched every inch of ground which she had covered during her walk, and the only thing that had occurred to her was that someone had found it; maybe mailed it— "God, I hope not!" she had said—and maybe hadn't mailed it.

She had pleaded: "Chad, couldn't you help me see if it's at the post office? Or couldn't I advertise in your paper? Anything to get it back!"

"My next edition comes out Monday," he had said. "That wouldn't be much help."

"The post office is closed, Chad."

"I know. I guess I can call Doc MacMillan and see if he can help you. Maybe someone did mail it."

"I have to have it, Chad."

"I'll try to help," he had said. "Maybe someone picked it up and will drop it off at your place."

She couldn't remember whether or not she had written a return address on the envelope.

Chad had dialed MacMillan and exacted from him a promise to watch out for the letter; all the while aware so keenly of her presence that he had had to swing his chair around and face the window while he spoke to the postmaster, and it was as he was doing so that he saw Poppy's car pull up out front.

Then, as he hung up, Delia Benjamin said, "I think I owe you some kind of explanation, Chad. I mean—" grinding out her cigarette with a determined gesture, "Oh, Lord, Chad, I'm sorry about what happened between us. I want you to know—"

He had had to interrupt her. "Poppy Porter's on her way in," he had said. "I'll put her off"; thinking, I've got to tell Cass myself that Benny was here, not let her hear it somewhere; thinking, now, finally, I'll know why Benny married him; now, finally— And rising to go to the door and head off Poppy out in the corridor, felt the sudden limpness through him, and his heart pounding in a crazy way.

Now he walked from the window and sat back down behind his desk. Benny was lighting another cigarette.

While her eyes were lowered and hidden from his face, he looked at her again, closely. He had the hollow thought. She was mine once. He had been a boy then; and now as a man he was jealous of that boy, and angry with him for losing Benny by some clumsy bungling. A bitter nostalgia enveloped him, and he did not want to believe that it *had* been his fault, his failing that was the reason she was not his now. He felt cheated—more cheated at that moment than he had felt the day she left him. And he knew then that fear was the only possible reaction he could have had seeing her again.

"Is Poppy happy?" she said, blowing a smoke cloud as she looked up at him again.

There's so much you don't know, Benny, he thought, so much I could never tell you, even if I were to fill you in on the years you were away; and those years sit between us in this room. Once we were young enough to push them aside and go on talking between ourselves; now we have let time and circumstances trap us, and we stall until we can see an opening in the wall. We tiptoe around yesterday in our stocking feet, afraid to wake it up-too soon. We say:

"Yes, Poppy's happy."

"I always liked Troy."

"He's running for the State Senate next term."

"No!"

He wanted to say, "Now, Benny. Tell me *why!*"

"She came to tell me about this fellow who's come to Bastrop because the high school's integrating on Monday," he said. "Just got a ride with him this morning out near—"

"Buddy!" she broke in suddenly. "My God, I'd completely forgotten!"

"You know him."

"He was with me this morning, out at the Dip! I forgot!"

"Then you *do* know him?"

She got up, tossing her cigarettes into her purse. "I left him there. He might have the letter. Oh, Chad, I completely forgot!"

Chad said, "Poppy said he was down at the Wheel."

"Yes, of course. Look, I'm going to hurry down there, and see if I can catch him. Do you want to come?"

"I don't think so," Chad said.

"Thanks," she said smiling, hurrying. "Thanks, Chad. It was good to see you again."

The door slammed shut behind her.

Chad sat staring at the cigarette butts in the ashtray, reached out and picked one up, touching the lipstick stain with his finger.

Buddy! she had said . . . *He was with me this morning, out at The Dip.*

She was back. . . . Now Jack Chadwick wondered why she had come back, and if she had come alone. She had seemed to know that this stranger would be speaking at the Wheel. *Yes, of course,* she had said.

He dropped the cigarette butt into the ashtray and sat there for a moment, hearing the rusty wall clock tick, and the fan's motor grind on the window sill. He leaned forward and rested his chin on his hands, and the note which Poppy had given him fell on the desk blotter.

Jud had said about the stranger: "He's from New York. A young fellow—doesn't look like a bum. Handsome, dresses well."

Chad picked up the wrinkled paper and unfolded it: It said:

ARNOLD BELDEN, IF YOU LET NIGGERS GO TO YOUR SCHOOL MONDAY MORNING, YOU WON'T SEE THE SUN SET MONDAY NIGHT!

WE WARNED YOU!

Chad said aloud: "God, Benny, no!"

PART SEVEN

". . . because the Nigra," the stranger continued, "is happy when he's living the way God intended him to live. The Supreme Court didn't create the Nigra, God created him, and God intended him to live the way he's inclined to live by his nature!

"Now there's a story," the stranger said, "about a visiting King who came to our country, and during his stay, took sick up in Washington, D. C. He was from a faraway land and he had one of those mysterious illnesses that is cured in a mysterious way. A spiritual way. He had his own doctor with him, and his own doctor told the President of our land, 'The King can get well only if he wears the shirt of the happiest nigger in the United States of America.'

"Well, folks," the stranger said, "we are a diplomatic people, and we are a friendly people, and we are an obliging people. So a search was inaugurated to find this happy nigger—the happiest one in our United States. And after a good deal of time—because we are a big land, and a heavily populated land—and because there are so many happy niggers living in this land, that it was no easy job finding the happiest. But after a good deal of time, he was located.

"Folks," the stranger said, "the President himself took that nigger, who was the happiest nigger in our land, into the White House, and up to where the King was sitting, sick.

"The President went into the King's room," the stranger said, "and he said 'King, I got the happiest nigger right outside the door. Shall I bring him on in?'

"The King said, 'I don't want him, I want his shirt,'" the stranger said. "'Bring me his shirt.'

"And then, folks," the stranger said, "The President had to tell him. He had to say, 'The happiest nigger in the United States doesn't have a shirt on his back!'"

A fat, shirt-sleeved, man shouted: "Just give him gin and chicken, s'all, and a chocolate bar to lick and hug!"

103

And behind him, another yelled: "What happened to the King? He still up in Washington sick?"

There was more laughter.

The stranger held his hand up again. "I'm glad you asked me that," he said, "because I'm going to tell you what happened to that King. He's still in Washington and he's still sick. He's very damn sick! And the President never knew what to do with him, so he gave him a seat on the Supreme Court."

The audience howled.

"The Supreme Court is sick!" the stranger said, "and going to school with niggers is sick!"

"Niggers are sick!" the fat man in shirt sleeves shouted. "Sick with syph—all of them got it. Everyone knows it!"

"Integration is sick!" the stranger yelled. "Do you know it is?"

A dozen or more yelled back. "Yes!"

"What is it?" Buddy asked.

The answer came. "Sick!"

"Niggers will be your brother first, and then your brother-in-law," the stranger said, "and what's that if it isn't sick?"

"It's sick!" the answer came.

"Integration is the first step toward mongrelization of the races!" the stranger said. "And how'd you like to see your daughter, or your sister, or your girl give her breast to a little black pickaninny."

"Sick!" was a roar now.

"Sick! Sick! Sick! the stranger's voice raised. "Niggers kissing whites! God, help me, don't let this happen in Bastrop! It's sick! What is it—you tell me—you people who live here—"

They told him, thundering their answer.

13.   *"A man gave me a present."*
                    —Johnny Chadwick

"W HAT MAN, darling?"

"A man in the back yard," the boy said. "He came in through the gate. I heard the gate squeak, and he said it was a present for me and I should go tell you."

Cass bent down and took the thin, square package from him. There was a black bow tied around white tissue paper. "Did he say who he was, darling?"

"Nope! Open it, Mama! What is it?"

"I don't know," she said, tearing the wrapping away. "Now, just be patient, honey."

"Maybe it's a clay set, Mama. Is it a clay set?"

In her hands Cass held a record folder, the sort that holds a thirty-three-speed record. There was a piece of brown paper pasted over the original cover, and at the bottom there was a crude drawing of a sheet done in white paint, with holes for eyes cut in it, and the three bold letters K.K.K. printed across it in black paint. Opposite that, there was a yellow-painted noose, hanging from a black tree limb.

"Is it, Mama?"

"Hush, honey, a moment—hush, Johnny-Bob."

Cass read the legend painted across the brown paper:

MUSIC FOR SWINGING NIGGERS

She stared at it, while Johnny-Bob tugged hard at her skirt.

"Mommie, please tell me."

"It's not a present," she said. "It's not a present, Johnny. It's just a joke.

"Why isn't it a present?" the boy whined. "The man said it was."

She reached inside the folder and felt a small seventy-eight-size record.

"Honey, run to the kitchen and ask Ginny Lee to give you some milk and cookies," she said.

"The man said it was."

"Please, Johnny-Bob, do as I say."

"I'd rather go back outdoors. I was building a house in the sand, Mama."

"I don't want you to go outdoors, Johnny," Cass Chadwick said. "I want you to go in and ask Ginny to give you some milk and some nice raisin cookies."

"It was wrapped like a present," the boy said, turning, starting toward the kitchen. "I felt the ribbon."

Standing in the hallway, Cass pulled out the record from its folder. It was a recording of "Dixie," and pasted to it was a note:

"You'll be hearing the same music, Chadwick, if you print any more in your rag about niggers going to school in Bastrop!"

". . . but it wasn't a present at all," she heard Johnny-Bob's voice from the kitchen. "It was just a joke."

Ginny Lee said, "Hoop! I saw dat dumb dope Suggs from de window. He slunk 'cross de yard like a suck-egg hound!"

PART EIGHT

". . . yes, they'd like to see it happen! The flat-chested, mannish women who wear pants and cut their hair like men and read books on Lenin! Yes, they'd like to see nigger boys teach innocent little white girls dirty things in the recess yard! And what's that? Hah? What's that?"

"Sick!"

"And the limp-wrist lavender boys that lisp-and wiggle like girls when they walk down the street. Yes! They'd like to see the nigger boys sitting in the classroom with their eyes watching the little white girls, watching the way they sit and waiting until they see something that'll get their nigger blood racing! What'll happen after school, hah? After school when they follow the little white girls home? Good, God-fearing people, I beg you to tell me, what kind of a situation is that? Tell me!"

"Sick! It's sick!"

"You know it's sick! Oh, Lord, you know it is! Help me! Don't let this happen. Yes, yes, the men that sit and pass laws that make little white girls have to be subjected to black nigger boys pushing them up against school lockers—yes, their little girls are grown up, and they don't care because their little girls are all grown up—those that were man enough to have any—and because now their minds are all they got left, and their minds have rotten thoughts. Yes, yes, their little girls are grown up, and they don't care a damn about the little girls in Bastrop, Alabama, who got to go to school on Monday with niggers! What do they care if the niggers smell and crawl with lice and know dirty words even I don't know, even you don't know, hah? What do they care! They passed a law, ladies and gentlemen, they say you got to abide by that law! I say that law is a sick law, and God help me, Lord God help me, I care about those little white girls! I'll fight for their honor! I'll defend their honor! God, help me, I'll kill that sick law! I'll kill that law! Help me to! I'm asking you to help me! I'm *asking you because that's a sick, sick, law! Do you know it?"*

"Yes!"

"Will you tell me? What is that law?"

"Sick!"

"Oh, say it!"

"Sick! It's sick!"

"God, yes, believe me!"

"It's sick!"

"Say it to the heavens. Let God hear you!"

"Sick, sick, sick!"

"Don't wait for me to ask you! Say it and say it!"

14. *"If the niggers start gettin' equal rights around here, might as well send manure to white schools too, and kiss cotton off for once and all."*

        —Duboe Chandler

THE CROWD across the street at the Wheel was still yelling and milling around under the ginkgo tree. Duboe stood outside Porter Drugs near Richard Buddy's car, and watched the stranger cross the street. There was almost no traffic along Court now; all who passed the Wheel in their trucks and cars had pulled over and parked, got out and listened—or stayed, leaning on their windows, watching.

The stranger was smiling as he approached. He clasped a hand on Duboe's shoulder.

"I got them going," he said. "I'll give them a rest for a while, and then I think you ought to take over."

Duboe said, "Hell, I ain't no talker. You are, though. You're great!"

"But now we need someone from here in town to talk," Richard Buddy said. "I got them worked up for you. You won't have any trouble."

"What the hell am I going to say! I ain't talked before a crowd."

"Tell them what you told me this morning. That's the stuff *I* can't tell them about. You know, Chandler, about the land getting poorer and the expense of fertilizer, and the way the niggers were living high off the hog back in forty-one when the Southwest was paying four cents more per pound of cotton."

"No one was living high off the hog, mister."

"Well, you know, Chandler. What you said this morning. It was you and your daddy running to the bank ass-licking for loans, and sitting up all night figuring out costs. The niggers were up all night drinking and screwing. It was the whites figuring out a way to make ends meet. Just tell them like you told me—if the niggers want equal rights so bad, how come they're willing to leech off the white man, and let the white man worry for them."

"People know that," Duboe said. "Everyone around here knows that. Hell, mister, we live with niggers! We know what they're like!"

"Chandler, to get these folks willing to go out and work for their rights on Monday morning, you got to remind them in every way you can think to that a nigger is a nigger, and that the Supreme Court up in Washington, D. C., is trying to make you people believe black is white."

Duboe said, "Well, I sure hate to get the niggers sore during in-season. It's a bad time to get niggers sore at you. They can slow up like nothing you ever saw 'less you saw a slowed-up nigger."

"If you give in to the niggers now, you might as well give up your place out there, Chandler. What the hell makes you think the niggers aren't going to slow up once they know they can go to school with whites? Let them niggers know their strength, Chandler, and you're going to have a thing happen here in Bastrop like what's happened down in Birmingham with the bus strike. Hell, the niggers can cripple you, if you give them an inch. You got to scare them, Chandler. Scare the living hell out of them!"

Duboe nodded slowly, "You got a point. Yeah, we got to keep them niggers in their places from the word go, or we ain't going to git nothing."

"So after a bit, you go on over and just talk to them. Just like you did to me this morning."

"Yeah," Duboe said. "You're right."

The pair stood watching the crowd. The stranger had left the pamphlets under the ginkgo, and people were grabbing them and standing in little groups reading them; passing them back to those in cars, shouting and discussing.

Duboe looked down Court and saw Delia Benjamin turning the corner on West Tennessee. She still strutted like a countess of some kind walking over the heads of prostrate serfs; long legs and long steps. He'd had his hands full with that behind she was shaking—once he had, when she was drunk and picked him up in the road that rainy night, and asked him where he was going. Duboe knew women; knew them well enough to know that if it was Ginny Lee Towers you wanted to jog, you took her out of the dump down at the Nelly, drove her to a view and conned her with candy-talk, until it was sweet like spring water and laughing in husky tones, until it was nice and you lie back sighing in the grass—smiling. But Delia Benjamin was a wildcat lay, and you didn't talk when you took the wheel and headed for the dump, down in the Nelly, and you didn't talk after, but in between you did, and she did, until she dug your back with her nails, and rode and cried; until it was silent and you heard her purse click and smelled the cigarette smoke. That one time.

The stranger said, "Here comes Dee."

"You know her? You work fast, mister."

"I'd like to know her."

"She wouldn't like this," Duboe said, pointing toward the Wheel. "She's uppity."

"A nigger-lover?"

"Her and her whole family. 'Cept her mother. Mother don't love anybody."

"What's Dee like?"

Chandler said, "Easy. Uppity but easy. Get her drunk first, though."

Richard Buddy smiled. "She's waving at me."

"Sure," Duboe said. "You're her type. She married a Northerner."

"I think I'll just—"

"Sure," Duboe said. "You go on and meet her." He chuckled, "A-yeah, get her drunk."

"I'll see you at your place at five-thirty," Buddy said, turning.

Duboe raised his hand in a mock "heil Hitler" salute: "Sick!" he said.

Richard Buddy clicked his heels and returned the salute. "Sick! Sick! Sick!" he said.

15.   *"... and now I'm afraid."*
                          —Arnold Belden

I MUST BE, Arnold Belden thought, or I wouldn't be here. He sat on the edge of the flower-splotched sofa uncomfortably, a thin, short man with a good head of white hair, deep brown eyes which were darting periodically from his hands to the mantle clock, and a lean, pensive countenance. It was the first time he had been in the Chadwicks' home, and he did not enjoy the fact that he was forced into a position in which he was obliged to be amiable with Jack. Cass, he admired—all the more as he glanced around the room and saw the vases of daisies and black-eyed Susans, the framed photographs of Johnny-Bob and Jack and herself which hung in various spots around the white wood walls, and the knitting bag beside the end table, the straw sewing basket in the corner; the books everywhere, and the unpretentious but comfortable Early American furniture. Cass, he felt, was a woman in the old-fashioned sense, unlike Poppy, who lived outdoors and had to be constantly on the go.

Where Jack was concerned, Arnold Belden neither particularly liked or disliked him, if he were honest with himself; but as a father who did not forget easily, and as a father who had resisted the urge countless times to kill Chadwick in cold blood, he would rather not have any occasion to be in his company.

Now there was such an occasion, and Arnold Belden sat there with Jud Forsythe and Jack and Cass, feeling as though he were going to blurt out, "There's no sense waiting for Poppy, Jack. She's not thoroughly insensitive, you know," because Poppy had told him about the visit with Jack. And afterwards, after Poppy took the twins and went home, Pam had said, "She isn't over him yet," in that matter-of-fact voice she used to say shocking things. "I've always suspected as much."

"It's eight-thirty," Jack Chadwick said, "Should we call again?"

Arnold Belden said, "Obviously Troy's not home yet."

"She could come alone, couldn't she?"

"She could," Belden said, "but I don't think she will."

"When I talked to her, she said she'd try."

What else could she say, Belden thought. Poppy's a cream-puff, not a Benjamin steamroller.

"I think we should go ahead," Jud said. "We can always call them tomorrow."

Chad stood by the mantle, spread-legged, smoking a cigarette. He said, "We've all been briefed on what's happened since noon. What we've got to do now is decide what we can do about it."

"I want to stay out of it," Cass said. "Monday morning I want to lock the doors and stay out of it."

Beyond the living room and the hallway, in the dining room, Ginny Lee Towers stood dusting the table, leaning forward so she could hear.

". . . whether or not we like it, we're already involved," Jud Forsythe was saying."

"Then let's not get more involved"—Cass Chadwick.

"Cass, let Jud talk!"

Ginny Lee clapped her hand to her mouth. Lawd, dat tole dat woman. She been in some state all day, Miz Cass, talking on de telephone wid her daddy. Nebber even tole Mister Jack she knew de whole time Miss Dee done marched herself in and paid de visit to his office. When Mister Jack say dis evening dat folks think Miss Dee in wid dis troublemaker stranger, Miz Cass jest sit on de chunk of ice. "Oh?" she say. "Really?" she say. Haw-de-daw, Gawd, he better tell her soon, or she gonna get de long puss and sleep in Mastah Johnny-Bob's room.

"Who is he anyway?" Cass Chadwick asked. "Someone Dee Benjamin brought down here!"

"We don't know that's true," Jack snapped.

"We know pretty well."

"We don't know that's true, Cass!"

Hee-haw, Gawd! You don't know you's walking in de quicksan, Mister Jack. Miz Cass daddy done told her what he saw down West Tennessee dis afternoon. You gonna need de heatin' pad in de bed t'night.

From behind her Ginny heard—"Psssss!"

She turned. "Nigger!" she hissed. "What yo' doin' in Mister Jack's? Yo' get outa here!"

Duggan Allen stood in the kitchen doorway. "You gets yo' hide out where I can talk, or I come in dere and drag yah."

"You nervy nigger!" she said, but she went toward the kitchen.

Out in the back yard, Duggan let go of her hand. "I like to kill you!"

"Mutual—*and*—mutual!" She stood up against the house, still carrying the duster.

"You was out wid Duboe at de dump last night."

"You was in dat dump, not me. De dump is for de rubbish, not me."

Duggan said, "Listen, I don't have time to argue wid you. Dere's trouble! Big trouble! De deacon says for everyone to come down to de church t'night at ten o'clock! White folks got eyes to make big trouble! Duboe got eyes!"

"I knows it! Dey's in dere talkin'."

"You go back and here what dey say," Duggan said. "And you be at de church with the information."

"I knows it!" Ginny Lee answered. "And Miss Dee was in to Mister Jack's today, and Miz Cass know it but—"

Duggan said, "You silly nigger, you listen! Don't care about Miz Cass business with Mister Jack. Dere's trouble, hear!"

"I hear. I knows it."

"You g'wan back and listen, and you be at de church. Tappy say you be dere too."

"I be dere."

"I got my own listenin-post 'tend to," Duggan Allen said. He darted back behind the tulip trees, on his way out and down the drive.

Ginny Lee went back up the porch steps, and paused. Someone was in the kitchen.

Jack Chadwick was saying, "Thank you for coming, Poppy. Here, I'll get the ice cubes. This always sticks."

"I wasn't going to come, and then—"

"Poppy, when you came to see me this afternoon, I was in a jam. Look, Poppy, Cass doesn't even know. Dee came to see me."

"I can get it all right," Poppy Porter said. "Here, give me a glass."

"I was upset, Poppy."

"I know you were. I just didn't know why. I thought it was—me."

"I knew you did. God, Poppy, I've always wanted to say something to you about—well, about how rotten I acted toward you. I wasn't myself then—after Benny left, I just wasn't."

"And now that she's back?"

"I don't know. Poppy, I plain don't know!"

"You know what they're saying. About this stranger and her."

"I can't believe it! Poppy, can you?"

"Troy's dad said they came into the drugstore this afternoon. Said they talked for an hour or so over a soda in back."

"Oh . . . Well, well—"

"It's hard to give up the old idol, Jack. *I* know. I used to think I'd never get over you. When the radio played love songs, I used to run all the way across a room and snap it off. Used to walk out of movies when there was any romantic scene. Gaw, I was in such a state, Jack."

"I'm sorry, Poppy. Sorry is all I can say."

"It was so boring," Poppy said.

"Huh?"

"Here's your glass, Jack. I said, it was boring. I finally woke up and realized I was bored to tears."

Jack Chadwick laughed, "Poppy, Poppy, you always make such sense, don't you? It is boring, isn't it? It is boring to be all wrapped up in the past."

"Up to a point," she said, "the past improves. The more you think about it, the better it seems. But if you keep at it as long as I did, pretty soon all the days you wasted thinking about it are in the past too, and you have to consider them."

"I'm glad you came, Poppy. I'm glad we had a chance to talk."

"We better go back now. Daddy's probably in there sure I'm having my heart broken out here in the kitchen."

"He doesn't still think that!"

"Daddy likes the idea of protecting his only daughter. With Troy taking such good care of me, he doesn't get much chance to think that way, so whenever he can, like right now—"

Jack said, "We'll go on in, and you better smile!"

"Jack," she said, "I hope you get bored! I pray God you do!"

"Thanks, Poppy," he said. "Thanks, girl."

The kitchen door swung shut after them.

Ginny Lee Polk Ann Towers wiped her face with the dust rag. Working dis house gonna make me a nervous wretch, she thought, hee-haw dong, roof gonna blow off any day de week now.

16. *Basically I'm a very nice guy . . .*
—*Richard Buddy*

I NEVER SAID you weren't," Dee answered, toying with the paper straw in her empty Coke glass, "but why are you so excited because the Negroes are going to school with the whites?"

After dinner at her house, they had driven out to Beggsom's Place because she said she didn't really feel like going into town. Richard Buddy wondered whether the real reason she had rejected his idea to go to a movie down at the Alabama was that she didn't want to be seen with him. The juke box was playing "I Could Have Danced All Night," and behind them, in back of the counter, John Beggsom was reading a newspaper and sipping a cup of coffee. They were the only ones there. Beggsom showed sense. While he nodded and said hello when they came in, he didn't act as though he knew Buddy at all. Every few minutes Buddy's arm shot across the table and gave her another light for another cigarette.

"Did you see the play?" she asked, not waiting for him to answer the other question.

"What play?"

"*Fair Lady*. The one this song is from. Maur and I saw it on opening night."

He was not pleased with the way the evening was going. She was always referring to her ex-husband. Even her mother had noticed.

Said, "Delia *dear!* Mr. Buddy doesn't want to hear about Maur all the time!"

And driving out here, when he had asked her where she'd lived in New York City, she had answered, "In the East Sixties."

It had infuriated him. She could simply have given her street address, or said "61st Street," "63rd"—whatever the street was, instead of inferring she was Miss Rich Bitch of all time.

He knew her type well enough. He had seen them walking jewel-collared poodles down Fifth Avenue, waiting under canopies for cabs or limousines along Park, huddling over frozen éclairs in mink-bedecked bands at Rumplemayer's, and sitting with supercilious arches to their carefully plucked eyebrows across the table from their well-tailored executive husbands, in the Pavillon, the Voisin, or the Oak Room. The rich, the privileged, the sick-chic few!

"I wouldn't go to a play on opening night," he told her. "It's vulgar." He knew a thing or two himself.

"Perhaps. It was a good play, though, Richard."

"I know the play." He laughed, thinking of the pamphlets. He'd spent his last cent on them. "I'm not arguing that the play isn't good. I'm just saying it's vulgar to go to opening nights." He remembered something his mother used to say, and he added. "It's as vulgar as wearing mink in the daytime. People with taste don't do that either."

"You're angry at so *many* things, Richard." She smiled, as if she were going to add, *poor baby*. He liked that about her. She seemed to sympathize with him, in some remote way. He couldn't be sure why it was—or *if* it was —but he felt something there every now and then. Some veiled affection for him, as though she understood him, or wanted to.

"I'm not angry, that's not the word for it, Dee. I'm just impatient with people who don't have good taste." He rubbed his thumb across the silver lighter. That lighter had cost plenty. He wondered if she recognized the fact that it was an expensive one, not a piece of junk. "And that answers your question too," he said "You ask more questions without waiting to hear the answers, Dee."

"I know. I'm sorry. Maur always says the same thing."

Maur again!

She took another cigarette from her pack on the table, tapped it and waited for the light he gave her. As he leaned forward he could feel the letter on his inside pocket, feel its edges, the fat long letter she had written this Maur. He had lied to her, told her that he hadn't come across it out at the Dip. He had intended to give it back to her

—he still wasn't sure he wouldn't—but for some perverse reason, perhaps because she seemed so eager to have it back, he kept it. He was torn between returning it to her and reading it, or finding a way to do both. But she had Scotch-taped it shut. It wouldn't be easy to read it without her knowing about it.

He had decided to see how the evening went—thought of driving her out to the Dip for another look; then, dramatically, producing it, as though he had just found it. It would be a way of getting her off alone with him, and it would be a subtle way of making her rather obligated to him, or grateful anyway. He had a bottle in the car. He could take it from there.

She said, "But all this talk about *niggers*, Richard. That's not in very good taste."

"That's a way of speaking," he said, "so that one can reach the mass mind. You know how that works. During the war, we weren't fighting the Germans. We were fighting the Nazis. And now, we aren't fighting the Russians. We're fighting the Reds."

"And the Negroes too?"

"No, Dee, not *the* Negroes. But the idea of integration. We're fighting the Negro who wants to blend with the white. The *nigger*."

"Richard, what's in it for you? Why do you care?"

"I'm a private citizen," Richard Buddy answered, "and I care the same way a lot of private citizens care about what happens to their country. Only I care enough to do something about it. Dee, it cost me money to come down here. No one paid me; it came out of my own purse. A man believes in something strong enough, he does something about it. Dee, remember that fellow who believed in world citizenship? He had his picture in *all* the papers."

She said, "Oh, yes. Vaguely. I didn't remember his name."

"Oh, Lord, yes—he was in *Time* and *Life* and the newsreels. Everything! Well, he believed in something enough to fight for it, too. Dee, I simply believe the Negro is better off segregated. That's the way I feel!"

"I suppose you're entitled to your opinion," she said, "and I guess you're entitled to make speeches about your opinion. But Richard, just a word of advice from an old Bastropian, hmm?"

"What's that?"

"You're in with a bad crowd. You may have very well-thought-out ideas about integration—I don't know. But the Chandlers—people like that—I saw you with Duboe out in front of Porter's this afternoon. Well, here in Bastrop they're just troublemakers."

He lit another of her cigarettes for her. "Listen, Dee," he said, "There was a crowd down there at the Wheel. A crowd! Not just the Chandlers, Dee, but a mob! Did you ever think that *you* might be in the minority?"

"I don't care one way or the other, really. I've been away too long. I'm not a fighter any more."

He thought: And you're soft now, after soft beds with the sheets changed daily; after soft silk and soft velvet; and soft living in the East Sixties; after sick, soft-soft, you don't have to fight.

He said, "I drew a big crowd, and I didn't get booed, Dee." I got cheered, he thought; God, I did!

"On Saturdays," she said, "the hill people come to town. A lot of people come to town Saturdays we don't see all week."

"I didn't think you'd try to belittle me, Dee."

She reached over and touched his sleeve. He wore a petulant expression—one he'd perfected that was a cross between an offended look and a disappointed one—the expression Lennie Gold used to call his "fey" look. Lennie used to say, "Don't act for *me*, please! I didn't pay to get in!"

Lennie was a goddam fool, trying to get his ass in med school so he could be another Freud. He'd fixed Lennie, goddam him.

"Richard," she said in an incredulous tone, "I wasn't belittling you. I was trying to explain a fact to you. You weren't talking to people in Bastrop. You were talking to people from around the country, from up in the hills, and off on farms. Backwoods folks, and white croppers."

He looked at her with his "searching" expression—one he'd perfected that was a cross between an interested, wondering look and a disappointed one—the expression that had made Lennie Gold blow his top that last afternoon they were together. Lennie had said: "Don't tell me you didn't report it, Richard, because I know you did! Don't give me that look! You were the only one who knew

I'd never paid state income tax! The only goddam one, Richard!"

Richard Buddy said to her, "Dee, you're something of a snob, aren't you? After your years in the East Sixties."

It worked. He could tell by the look in her eyes.

After she got through denying it, he'd suggest helping her find the letter.

He looked at the clock on the wall of Beggsom's Place. Nine-ten.

At nine-ten, Jack Chadwick stood in the hallway between the living room and the dining room. As he listened to Doris Towers voice over the telephone, he could hear Cass's in the other room.

" . . . that when Crabb Suggs come into my back yard and goes up to my child, I'm plenty scared! What if something should happen to Johnny-Bob as a result of all this! No, you can say all you want, Jud, about duty and responsibility to the Nigra, but I'm thinking about my own!"

Poppy answered her, "Don't you think I haven't got kids, Cass? That's why Jud's right! If Crabb Suggs and his kind take over around here, our kids aren't going to have a safe—"

Cass interrupted her: "Is that really why you think Jud's right, Poppy? Or is it because Jack suggested the idea in the first place!"

Damn her, Jack thought! God damn her. She was on some kind of morbid tear tonight, and she didn't care who she ripped into.

Into the phone's mouth, he said, "Doris, you tell your people that we're going to do everything we can to see that there's no violence on Monday. I know there've been threats. I know it. I've been threatened myself. But I'll guarantee you—" Jack Chadwick said . . .

"I'll guarantee you," the young man with the brush cut said, sitting in Julius's down in Greenwich Village that Saturday night at nine-ten, "that wherever he's gone, he's causing trouble."

The Negro with him bit into his hamburger. "He just likes to talk big, that's all! He's just a character, going off like he was on some kind of secret mission." He laughed. "He's a character."

"He's not very funny, if he is. Look, Artie, I know that guy. I roomed with him. He's never gotten over the fact he was rich once, and then suddenly he wasn't rich. His old man went bankrupt, and little ole Richard had to go to work. He's never gotten over it. And when he went to work, he couldn't hold down a decent job because he knew it all. Had a goddam Napoleon complex! Once he had a job up at Crub & Corrigan, writing copy. His boss called him down once on something and our boy Richard screams at him, 'Don't be impudent to me! Don't you dare be impudent to me!' And when the boss canned him, our boy picks up a bottle of ink, takes off the top, and turns it upside down on top of the boss's desk . . . Artie, when he told me about it, his eyes were blazing like he had a fever, and he said to me, 'Lennie, I know something that's going to ruin that Mr. Havermayer. Something about the way he voted back in forty-eight. I just think some of C.&C.'s clients might be interested.'"

Artie said, "He just talks, Lennie. Richard's all right, boy. My sister was sure soft on him."

"Sure," the brush cut said. "He used to love to go where Vie was singing, didn't he? Loved the way she sang right to him and everyone looked. Loved the way she came and joined him after at the table. Old attention-starved Richard. Killed him 'cause he lost his money! I was with him one night down on Jones Street when he sprained an ankle kicking the side of a Cadillac. He was yelling 'I could have had this nothing! This nothing! I could have had a whole fleet of nothings like this!'"

"I think he really liked Vie," Artie said. "They were sweet on each other a long time."

"Until she ditched him. Then he wasn't so sweet. Remember the night he stood right here, Artie, right by the bar, and yelled at her? Remember? 'I'll get even, you— nigger,'" he said.

"Aw, he was hurt, Lennie. You know Richard. Blows a lot of steam off."

"Ever hear his ambition? Told me one night when he was drunk."

"He used to tell me he thought he might go into politics. He did a lot of speech-making, remember? He was all right."

Lennie Gold said, "He just liked to hear himself talk. Liked to get upon those sound trucks and shoot his big mouth off. Naw, his ambition, Artie, the way he told me, was to be on the cover of *Time*."

"Nothing wrong with that, Lennie. You just got a chip, boy."

"I just got a stomach-full, Artie. That's all."

At nine-ten Mrs. Gus peeked from the crack in the doorway at the men sitting around the kitchen table. Goodness, some of them she didn't even know; never saw before in her life, and when she made notes it was hard to distinguish one talker from the other.

Big-nose said: "Naw, now I don't go for sending any kind of threatening note to Jud. Hell, Jud—he ain't just a Sunday-in-the-pulpit-Christian. He come out to my place last winter, when Irie took down with arthritis, and—"

Gus Chandler interrupted, "I don't have anything against Jud either. Like him all right. But if Duboe's right and he's meeting down to Chadwick's with all of 'em—"

"Hell," Big-nose said, "we don't even know what's going on down there."

"Well, Duboe will be back soon," Crabb Suggs said. "But Jud Forsythe ain't gonna be on our side. A note don't hurt none. A good strong note, to let 'em all know we ain't going to have no interference on Monday when we meet them niggers going to school."

"I say leave Jud out of it," Big-nose said.

"It's his church the young folks go to, and it's them giving us trouble." Suggs said. " 'S the goddam Episcopalians! Progressive element!"

Mrs. Gus threw her pencil down and wandered over to her bed. She picked up the soap and smelled it.

"I got a notion they'll ask me on Monday," she said, "and I'm going to *refuse!* I'm going to tell them they can have their old smelly soap!" she said. "I'll tell them all!"

Behind her, someone pulled the door shut. The men's voices were muffled now so that she couldn't hear.

". . . sick in bed about it," Flo Benjamin was saying at nine-ten, "because he seemed right nice, Gay. I was even going to offer to have him spend the night down in the guest room and all . . . Huh? . . . Well, law now, Gay, wha'm I going to *do?* Law, we didn't have no way of knowing all that! He no more seemed like the type to stir up *vi*-o-lence than the man in the moon! Law, Gay, wha'm I going to *do?* She went off with him, and I got my hair all up and all, I'm jest sick in bed about it!"

". . . but first, we going to pray," Deacon Phillips said down at Bastrop Baptist Union in the Nelly, "and first, we going to sing!"

"And then, we going to organize!" Turner Towers said from the front row, "because how long we going to pray!"

The deacon was firm. "We going to pray first!"

"How long? Deacon, how long?"

"Until we're through, Brother Towers," the deacon said.

"We going to pray crow and eat crow, Deacon!"

"Oh, Lord—"

"I mean it, Deacon! We've got to organize!"

From a back row, old black Tappie Towers said, "The deacon say 'Oh Lord,' big mouth!"

"I said, Oh, Lord," the deacon said.

"Oh, Lord," the congregation said.

"Oh, Lord, let our words fall gently—"

"Let our words fall gently—" the congregation said— *on the white woman, Rastus, don't fall on the white woman.* . . . "And oh, Lord, and oh my God," the deacon said—at nine-ten.

17.   *". . . just tell Dee I called."*
                                    —Maur Granger

. . . "is exactly what I *won't* do," Flo Benjamin said aloud, driving down State I at ten that night, curlers poking out from under the green and yellow bandanna she had wrapped around her head. Don't know why all this has to start right at a time so important. Gay Porter been trying to even things off ever since I was made Terpsichore, and tonight she got her chance. Dee out parking with someone violent and the whole town talking. Didn't seem violent. Knew to take the right fork at dinner and all, but Maur was the same way. No way on earth of telling he

was Jewish. Smart New Yorker. Calling Delia up when
he was divorced to her and all. Probably drunk. Saying:
"Hello, Mrs. Benjamin," just as bold as you please. "Is
Dee home?"

Told him. "My daughter is out at a party, Mr. Granger.
She will not be in at an early hour this evening."

Felt safer now that the dial phones were in. Operators
didn't listen in. 'Course, the long-distance ones did. There
wasn't any protection there. But Gay's call wouldn't be
all over town.' Then facing that filthy John Beggsom in
curlers. Gaw, that girl don't care how she humiliates me;
never did! And him saying: "I reckon they went off to
spark somewhere, Mrs. Benjamin!"

Flo Benjamin slowed her car down as she approached
the Dip. The moon was bright.

It was so bright that Duboe could see her plain as anything when she started down Love Lucy.

"Hey!" he said, "you snubbing me." He grinned at her
from his car. "Hey you, Ginny Lee."

She stopped and squinted at him. "Duboe, that you?"

"C'mere," he said. "I know some dirt on Mr. Jack. He
had a visitor today."

"That's dumb old stupid dirt," she said. "I knowed that
two clock s'afternoon, from de same source you knowed
it. He called up to de house and tole Miss Cass."

"C'mere just the same," he said. "C'mon, gal. You don't
have to go to the meeting. They only singing down there.
A-yeah, they singing all about hallelujah, the blood done
signed my name. That's what—just singing."

"I'm glad you remind me the fact," she said, "'cause
it remind me other facts, troublemaker!"

He giggled. "You like my troublemaking! You know
it!"

"Not the kind you making with Crabb Suggs and yo'
daddy and dat stranger from up North. No one like dat
kind, troublemaker!"

"Mister Jack didn't have no meeting about it, though.
Mister Jack don't have the sense to have a meeting."

"Not a little meeting, no! A big one! And you all ain't
going to get nowhere come Monday, troublemaker!"

Duboe said, "Mister Jack's too dumb to figure out anything to stop us."

"Haw, gaw, dat all you know. You dumb if you think it! Mister Jack and Mister Jud and Mister Troy going to. *escort* any colored. goin' to school, personal!"

"You making it all up, Ginny Lee. A-yeah, you just tell big old stories all the time to try and scare Duboe."

Ginny Lee Polk Ann Towers strutted over to the car with her hands on her hips. "That's all you know you so stupid and dumb," she began, "because I heard everything said at that meetin'——"

"I wish you'd think things through and not always act on impulse!" Troy Porter said.

He set his drink down on the end table with a bang and got up, paced back and forth across the front room.

"I did think it through!"

"Well, while you were thinking, Miss Einstein, did it ever occur to you that I'm a politician! I'm not trying to sell newspapers, same as Jack, and I'm not trying to sell God, same as Jud, I'm trying to sell myself to my constituents, every single living one of whom lives in Alabama —not just in Bastrop, but in the state of Alabama! In the South, Poppy!"

Poppy said, "I don't see how I hurt anything, Troy."

"I know you don't," he thundered, "and that's what makes me all the damn madder! Poppy, do you know that the Birmingham *Post-Herald* had a picture of what went on at the Wheel in their late edition?"

"Well, what does that matter?"

"Now you just think about this for a minute," he said, reaching for his drink and pointing it at her. "You just think how it'd look if I'd been down there on the courthouse lawn yipping hooray with the rest of the crackers. You thinking about that, Poppy?"

"It'd look awful. I think it'd look horrible."

"But I'm telling you the facts of life, Poppy. A picture of me down there yipping hooray this afternoon on the courthouse lawn, as horrible as it might seem to you or me, wouldn't lose me enough votes in the state of Alabama to even put a dent in my winning ones. It wouldn't do me no good, maybe, but it'd sure not hurt me the way a picture of me leading niggers to school would! Did you ever think about that when you were promising me away to good causes? Did you ever think how a picture of me leading niggers to school would look to the people who're going to elect me, pray God, elect me, to the senate of the State of Alabama? Huh? Did you?"

There was the sound of ice cubes swimming in the bourbon as he raised the glass to his lips and swallowed. Then silence and the moon for a spotlight on Poppy's chair.

"For one thing," Jack Chadwick said, sitting on the bed, slamming the shoe he unlaced to the floor. "You're jealous! Jealous of everyone and everything! Talking to Poppy that way—Gawd, Cass! There's something wrong with you! And for another thing—" throwing the other shoe—"you're a Beggsom!"

"What does that mean, Jack?"

He said, "That means what it says. You know your old man is in with Suggs and Chandler and the whole lot of them." As he said it, he had the satisfaction of knowing that this, more than anything else, would goad her, and he realized he wanted to shame her in some way, for her conduct that evening. She had behaved like a shrew, lambasting everyone in that way of hers, that simply chucked reason, discretion and logic out the window, and employed a more personal attack. Sentences would begin: "Well, Jud, I know you *once* were a family man, but now —" and end ". . . because I wonder, Poppy, if you're more interested in the publicity than in the welfare of the Nigra children."

Jack remembered the stories that had circulated about Cassie's mother. "Beggie" they'd called her in Bastrop; said she was a little "teched;" used to boil up scalding water when she was mad at old John, and go after him with it, chasing him down the hill in their old Ford, and running on foot when he broke from the road, dragging the pail and cursing at him. Cassie never knew her, but old John talked "Beggie" all the time when Cass was a child. Said: "Beggie wouldn't take no guff!"

"Beggie put her own over God!" and "Beggie worked hard, loved hard, lived hard, laughed hard, and died doin' somethin' about the population. Fought her way in, out, and all through life, an' don't shame her purpose."

Jack watched his wife slip off the linen dress and reach for the hanger in her closet; thought: She come a long way from Beggie and Old John, mostly on her own, come; and suddenly he was tired of the petty picking at one another. He began to say, "It's pretty silly to fight this way," but got only to pretty before Cass said: "Daddy isn't mixed up in this. I know that for a fact . . . But Delia Benjamin is."

"Who's talking about her?"

"I am!" she answered emphatically. She was bending down to pick up slippers. "I've never brought her name up unfairly. I've never done that, Jack, you've got to admit I haven't. Never tried to bring her name up or imply anything about her. Have I? You'll admit that, won't you?"

Jack knew a hundred ways this was preposterous, untrue and beside the point. He said, "I can't see how Benny enters into this discussion one whit."

"Benny! The special little white bah lamb with the special little blah-bah name!" Cass Chadwick said, snatching her robe from the closet, "And this is not a discussion! This is a fight! A low-down, below-the-belt, name-calling blowup! But if we're going to discuss anything, let's begin with why Delia Benjamin went to see you this afternoon, and let's continue with why you didn't bother to bring it up this evening!"

"Stop yelling," he said. "you're going to wake Johnny-Bob up." He rubbed his eyes with his knuckles. God, would Benny's name ever just leave him blank? Would a time come like that? "This narrow-minded, ninny little town," he said, "I'm fed up! I hate it!"

He probably loved Bastrop better than anyone living there, and he knew it. The same way the "real" New Yorkers, the bona-fide Manhattan romanticizers were uprooted from places like Ida Grove, Iowa; White River Junction, Vermont; Naples, Italy—a generation back, or Geneva, New York; Newark, Ohio—adopting New York; becoming its adopted son. As he was here in Bastrop, after years of youth spent wandering in cities; then as a young man finding the small town he'd known existed from reading Sinclair Lewis novels, and the "home," the "girl next door." Not quite, Benny; but oh, we were "it" just the same! Me and Benny.

Cass said, "That's a good answer. It's the town's fault." She walked over and sat down at her dressing-table mirror. "If the town would only leave you and Delia Benjamin to yourselves, everything would just be ducky, wouldn't it?"

"All right," he said, "she came to see me." *I'm back, Chad,* that fear-filled time that ached with the insufficiency of any drama, and too much beauty-pain, and memory.

"I know *that.*"

"Look, Cass, she lost something, see? She lost a letter and she came to see me," he said; from across years through doubt and impotent wonder, stepping into today more suddenly than the shock of seeing her last night, to say, "I lost a letter."

"Because you're the Lost and Found Department. Well, that makes some sense. Umm-hmmm. What else?"

"If you'd stop rubbing grease all over your face, I'd tell you what else! She came about a letter she lost! Pure and simple. She said she didn't know who else to go to! I didn't ask her to come!"

"Why didn't you tell me?"

"I was going to." Maybe I was, he thought.

He got up from the bed and went across to her in his stocking feet, kneeling by her vanity chair. "This is silly, Cass. This is silly. She doesn't mean anything to me. I knew you'd be upset if I told you she'd visited me?"

"Oh, you did, ah? Why did you think that?"

He saw the stubborn dent in her chin. There would be no use to explain, he knew; and that was all right too. He would have trouble explaining himself if Cass were listening to him in a reasonable frame of mind.

"Never mind," he said, "we won't discuss it."

She said, "I'm not going to be made a laughingstock all over town."

"What? Cass, what are you talking about? She just came to see me!"

"You know the Nigras learn things first," she said; "they always do. Well—" she screwed the jar of cold cream tightly with a quick jerk to her arm—"tonight Ginny made the bed up in Johnny-Bob's room before she left!"

"She's just crazy!" Jack said. "She probably heard us arguing and took a notion to do it."

Cass said, "She never did it before!"

Then she kicked back the vanity chair and aimed the

cold cream jar at the three-winged dressing-table mirror.

"Benny!" she said above the noise of shattering glass. "Damn her guts!"

Out on the front porch of the Benjamins', Dee sat beside him in the glider, the big red moon giving light to them—their drinks on the round tin table, his long legs stretched out in front of him, shoes kicked off; and her own heels set side by side near the wicker chair, her legs drawn up under her. He had managed to get very drunk.

". . . when it came the day to auction my folks' house up," he said, "I fixed myself some dinner in the kitchen. There was only some old dehydrated soup there, and I boiled it up for dinner. I remember when I poured it out into the bowl, there were bugs swimming in it. Must have come from the soup that was years old, and only the maids ate anyway. I ate the soup anyway, I remember. I kidded about it. Better get used to bugs in the soup, boy, I kidded myself, and bugs in the beds, cause the money's all gone. Pffttt!"

He took a swallow of the Scotch, and leaned back against the glider. "We were rich once, Dee. R-i-c-h!" Another swallow, finishing what was in his glass. "Are you drunk?" he asked.

She said, "No."

"I'm not either," he said.

She got up, "I'll make us another. Don't know where Mama could be. Never known her to go out and leave the lights burning before." She passed in front of him, "I won't be a minute."

Now she thought: how can I get rid of him? She felt tired and longed to be free to run a hot bath to soak in before bed. Buddy's speech was getting thick, and he had already become fixed in that aura of utter self-absorption which Maur used to call the: "I never knew why nurse took teddybear away" mood—"until *one day.*"

God, she missed Maur!

"I'll come too," she heard behind her. "I'll help you."

He walked somewhat unsteadily, leaning into a table as he passed.

"Okay?" she said. She waited while he came to the kitchen door.

He stopped and looked at her, looked fully at her, slowly.

She was caught between being amused by him, or annoyed with him. He was handsome and ingenuous and incredibly obvious.

"Why didn't you want to go out to the Dip?" he said.

"I told you. It would be pointless. If I couldn't find the letter by day, I certainly couldn't find it by night."

"Are you drunk yet?" he said.

"No, but *you* are, Richard. I think we better call it a night, all right?"

"So you're a nigger-lover," he said. "Well, well, well . . . A rich nigger-lover."

His eyes were narrowing in a peculiarly vicious way which gave his whole face a new cast. Dee was fascinated with the change. He seemed to have disintegrated suddenly, like a Dorian Gray, and now he seemed no longer young or good-looking or naive, but like some seedy teen-ager who looked too old for his age, too nasty and clever in an ugly sense.

"I'm going to kick you out now, Mr. Buddy," she said. "The bar is closing."

"We're beginning to catch on to each other, aren't we?" he said. "Finally!"

"Maybe we are," she said. "Give me your glass." She reached for it. "I'm going to rinse them out and go to bed. The party's over."

"Why don't you scald mine. Might have germs."

"Oh, come on, Mr. Buddy," she said. "Richard, boy, give me the glass and let's not play gangbusters any longer. I'm tired."

He reached across and caught her arm, yanking her away from the kitchen door so that it swung shut behind her. They were in the hallway, an he pushed her away from the living room in the direction of the unlighted dining room. In her other hand she was carrying her glass, and she threw the melting ice from it toward him.

Instantly he slapped the glass out of her hand.

"Who do you think you are?" he said. He took hold of her shoulders. "Who in hell do you think you are?"

She looked at his face. He was perspiring and his eyes were bright and narrowed and angry. She didn't answer him.

"Who in hell do you think you are?" he said "You tell me that?"

She said nothing still.

Again he shook her shoulders against the wall. The china in the dining room bureau rattled. She heard him hoik and felt the wet spittle on her cheek.

"That'll show you," he said.

"Show me what?" She hadn't meant to speak.

"I can spit on your kind," he said. "Nouveau riche! Is this barn here your ancestral manor! Is it? I can spit on it—" again he spat—"I ought to teach you a lesson."

"You're hurting my arm, damn you—"

"Who do you think you are to look down on me; Who? You're sick, did you know that? You think that sick Plaza Hotel is important, don't you? It's a sick, sick place, and it's dull and stupid and vulgar! It's vulgar!"

He shoved her against the wall again. "I'll fix you," he said, "I'm going to fix you—"

He put his hands on her at the exact moment Flo Benjamin burst through the kitchen door brandishing an eggbeater.

Then later, after he had run to his car, his shoes thrown at him by Dee's mother, as she berated him in a squeaky high voice which was shaking with the tumultuous indignation of outraged Southern womanhood, Dee realized something that sent sudden fear through her.

She had never mentioned the Plaza to him. She had never told him that that was where Maur was living now.

18.

MORNING

came early down at Suggs's store; twenty after seven, in the back room, the sun kept from entering by the crust of filth on the windows, and Duboe laughing: "Hell, I'd ever seen this here supply room, Crabb, I'd buy my stuff over to Towers nigger heaven myself. Whew-wee, this shore is a seedy hole, man!"

"Sure," Suggs said, " 'cause I lost my best business since the nigger opened his nigger store. Can't even afford help!"

Gus Chandler hated being up at this hour; on a Sunday

looked forward to going back and getting more sleep. "We all know what we're supposed to do," he said. "I can see my names from the county s'afternoon. They'll all show up on Monday."

Duboe said, "Even in in-season, Pa?"

"Hell, enough'll show to scare the niggers. What the hell we need?"

"I ain't worried about enough to scare the niggers," Duboe said. "I'm worried about them dad-dum state troopers—somethin' like that. The guard or somethin'. What if they get called in?"

"They won't," Gus answered, tapping the dottle out of his pipe. "They won't because they don't think them that was in at the Wheel on Sunday will be around on Monday. They figure it'll be just a dozen or so of us kicking up."

Suggs said, "At the most, maybe they'll swear in Chadwick or Troy Porter, or some others as deputies. Nothin' bigger than that."

"Where's Buddy, anyhow?" Gus Chandler said.

"Sleeping off last night," John Beggsom laughed. "They was out to my place earlier in the evenin'—him and Easy-Dee."

"Lord, I just hope he got her drunk 'fore she got him drunk," Duboe said. "She can drink Texas."

At seven twenty-three in the morning prayer ended. Jud sank back in the throne chair on the altar while the choir sang:

> *My father, for another night*
> *Of quiet sleep and rest,*
> *for all the joy of morning—*

and he saw her then.

An usher escorted her to a pew near the front; and he saw her face, under the immense black picture hat, look up at him—look straight into his own with the same serious eyes he used to see everywhere when he shut his and let the darkness make dreams, and then he saw her head bow, and the white gloves touch the pew's back in front of her as she knelt:

> *Now with the newborn day I give*
> *Myself anew to thee,*

and he thought, welcome back, Delia. But then someone had joined her.

Jud recognized the stranger. He could feel the familiar murmur and rustle of the congregation that came whenever something was wrong; and he saw heads turn, heard the coughing. Always there was the coughing at a time like this, at ten-fifty in the *"Morning"* he said to her, kneeling beside her.

"Where did you come from?"

"From your house. I followed you. I want to talk to you."

She said, "You know I want it back, and I intend to get it back."

"Shhh," he said, "the lady with the yellow eyes two seats over is about to lose them out of her head. I like you because you're smart, Dee," he whispered. "How'd you know?"

She sat back in the pew, her program covering her mouth. "The Plaza," she said. "You mentioned it and I never had. But the letter was addressed there. Where is it?"

"I mailed it," he smiled.

"You're a damn liar," she said.

"Shhhhh, Delia," Richard Buddy whispered. "I'm sick in bed about the language you use in church."

of quiet sleep and rest,
for all the joy of—

"Morning," Flo Benjamin said to Senior and Gay out front of Second Methodist Church. "Isn't it a lovely Sunday morning?"

"We thought Dee might come along with you this morning," Gay said, "I was saying to Senior only just a minute ago, wonder why Delia didn't join her mama for service?"

"Oh, the young folks are partial to Jud, now, and you know that s'well as I do, Gay. Law, Dee got herself up with the birds to get all dollied up for the Episcopalians."

"I was just hoping," Gay said, "everything come out all right last night. Mmmm? Did everything?"

"As it turned out there was nothing at all to worry about," Flo Benjamin said. "Dee wasn't even with him, as it turned out, but home the whole time."

"Law, no, really?" Gay exclaimed. "What you know about that?"

"It sure is lovely," Flo Benjamin said walking along now, it sure is a lovely *morning*."

"*Morning*," Jack Chadwick said passing Cass on his way to the bathroom.

She said: "*Morning*. Cold with the sun cut and it up in the nineties at noon."

19.

AFTERNOON

JUST after noon, he looked up and saw her in the doorway of the vestry, just as he was changing.

"Jud? Hi," she said, walking across the thick gray carpet, offering her hand. "Thanks." She smiled when he felt the touch of her again. "I know you didn't have to do that. Everyone would have liked it better if you hadn't."

That was true. He said, "That's not true, Dee." He finished yanking off his clerical collar, reaching for the tie over the arm of his leather high-back chair. "Everyone's glad you're home again. I just made it official."

"Put the tie on," she said, "then tell me what in hell is wrong, Jud? Will you tell me that?"

He slipped the tie under his shirt collar and waved his hand at the couch near the window. "Is someone waiting, or can you sit down, Dee?"

"*Someone*," she said, "was just arrested." Reaching in her bag for a cigarette, she walked across to the couch. "For a minute I thought they were going to arrest me, too. What is it with everyone Jud? When you stood up there and said you'd like to welcome back Deila Benjaman, I could swear I heard the hair bristling! And suddenly everyone had colds and St. Vitus dance and ants crawling over them! I felt like Fatty Arbuckle or Carry Nation at a bartenders' convention."

"No," Jud said. "You felt like someone who was with Fatty Arbuckle or Carry Nation at a bartenders' convention."

She lit her cigarette and inhaled. "So that's it."

He watched her from where he sat, remembering that he had taught her how to inhale—and lots more. How to dance, how to drink so she could stand the taste of liquor, and how to make love.

She had thrust him into a long anguish through years of picking him up and setting him down like some rainy-day toy; smiling on him for favors and frowning on him out of boredom; letting him wind his long, love-trembling legs around her impassive body in any way he knew how, with her body marked off like a play court of some serious sport—the foul lines and the out of bounds—and always in the heat of his own passion and in the unbelievable lack of it in her reactions, she would interrupt to change the radio station and get better music; and ultimately after their clothes were twisted and gapping and wet with the perspiration of his dear work, she would say: *Jud? Hadn't we better start back?*

Then Chad came, and he had thought it would end there.

Delia Benjamin said, from the couch: "What I don't understand is all the heroics, Jud?"

What I'll never understand, Jud thought, is why she decided on it after Chad went off to war. What made her come to him that day, and say that?

"Heroics?" he said. "Dee, this fellow—whoever he is— has stirred up a lot of trouble. I don't think you realize."

"He's against the Negroes going to school—well, so are a lot of people," she said, "and he's made speeches down at the Wheel, and he's damn uncouth. But after all, Jud— since when do we arrest someone for that? Oh, I've got my own bone to pick with him, a good meaty one. But after all—"

She had said simply: *Jud, do you still love me? You always claimed you'd never stop.*

"Have you seen the pamphlets he's distributing?" Jud pulled open his desk drawer. "I've got one here you can look at." He got up and walked over to the couch, handing one to her. "He's been behind all the threats people have been getting, too," Jud said. "They're too clever— most of them—in their wording and presentation, for folks around here, in sympathy with him, to think of. Look at that."

Yes, you know I love you, he had said.

Then take me out tonight, Jud. Will you?

And it was crazy the way he knew exactly what she meant; just didn't know why. Never did.

He watched her face in its growing concern and faint alarm rising in the features now: "You've been away a long time, Dee," he said. "You've forgotten how things like this can pull the trigger on all the guns people have always had loaded around here. You've forgotten about the rednecks who hate the townspeople because credit's hard for them to get in the stores, or the poor whites who are even worse off than the Negro and blame the Negro for it—*hate* him! Or the backswoodsman who just plain likes any old lawless uprising that can help him blow off steam; or the farmer, Dee, who believes in keeping the Negro in his place as fervently as I believe in keeping Sunday sacred, and who'll go against any law that goes contrary to that belief! You've forgotten about these loaded guns back in the closets, a lot of us had—but they were always there. And now this fellow's managed to pull the triggers!"

Jud sat down beside her on the couch. And maybe, he thought, you've forgotten the old Negro woman's shack outside Morrow and the rain-racked night afterwards on the weeping-ride home through the vine-hung back roads; *you should have seen it, Jud, she showed it to me, held it up with her black hands, like a little wet rat. And it was a boy! Did you know you could tell at three months? Our son, Jud, and she put him down the hole in the out-house behind the place . . .*

"And I managed to meet him—first thing," she said looking up from the pamphlet. "Lord, how do I always manage to go head-first toward trouble, Jud?"

"You have a knack for it, I guess."

She put her head down: "God, I wish I'd never come back here!"

"Dee—" he touched her hair—"don't feel that way," he said, feeling that way himself, wishing she'd never come back; like an albatross, he thought, for the first time thought that in *how* long?

"I wish I'd never come back," Troy Porter said after dinner that afternoon, as he sat out on Belden's back porch, watching the twins play on the lawn. "I was thinking of staying in Montgomery through Monday, but I hated to leave Poppy alone. Now, this mess!"

"Pam and I understand your position," Arnold Belden told him. "I want you to know that, Troy. Poppy ought to know a man can't be a politician and a hero at the same time."

"Oh, now, I wouldn't put it that way, Arnold." Troy leaned forward in the wicker chair, frowning. "I mean, I never *was* for integration, you know that. So why should I lead the Nigra kids to school? I mean, look at it that way. I've always had a very clear picture of how I felt about the Nigra. You know, Arnold, during the war when I was laid up outside Cannes, I met up with the Towers boy, right in the same hospital. Uniform and all. I had my leg busted and I was sitting out on the porch and they brought him out to me—this French boy did. Had the idea we'd be thrilled to see each other because we were from the same home town. You know, Arnold, that colored boy was just plain miserable out there talking to me. I tried to put him at his ease best I could, but you know the Nigras feel stronger about what's proper even than we do. He just didn't feel right, Arnold. Felt things were way out of proportion. I could tell. Way after the war I met him in the drugstore—I was with Poppy, and he was back to himself again, back to normal. All smiles and wanting to know if he could take care of any odd jobs around the house." Troy bit off the end of a cigar and struck a match. "I tell you, for the Nigra's sake, as well as for what I believe is right, I oppose integration."

Arnold said, "Well, that's not exactly the point being made, Troy. It's the law now. It's whether we go by it, or go against it."

"Oh, I'll go by it," his son-in-law answered, sucking smoke through the cigar, "but I can't see helping it be enforced. That's not my job."

Arnold thought a moment, studying his nails. He said finally, "That's not the point, either, Troy. It's just that we seem to be in trouble in Bastrop. Jack Chadwick thought—"

Troy Porter pulled his cigar out of his mouth and said sharply: "And I'm sick of what Jack Chadwick said!"

"We all thought," Arnold Belden said quietly, "that it'd be a way to counteract the trouble!"

Troy didn't say anything.

"Pam and I understand your position," Arnold Belden said.

"I wish *I* did," Troy answered. "I wish I knew what I'm supposed to do tomorrow. Here's my father-in-law threatened, and my neighbors threatened, and Poppy promising my career away to a Nigra escort service, and a reporter from the Birmingham *Post-Herald* down at the hotel. I wish I knew what I'm supposed to do. I did the one thing I thought would help—got that Yankee locked up. But what'm I supposed to do tomorrow?"

"Pam and I understand your position." Arnold Belden had said that too many times already.

But the third time it didn't irk Troy because he was thinking of something else now; something he could do about that position by just making one phone call.

"Afternoon is nice, Daddy," the boy said, standing by the oak. "Is this brown?"

"That's brown," Jack Chadwick answered. "Smell the air, son? Smell the brush burning? Well, those leaves are all colors—red, like the sun is hot; and green, like grass feels, and yellow, like lemons smell, and brown—"

"Like the tree," the boy said.

"Yes, like the tree. And when folks rake them up and burn them, all those colors smell like the air, Johnny, like it smells now. Isn't that a good smell!"

"I want to make Mommie a necklace," the boy said. "Can I?"

Jack bent over and picked up some leaves. "C'mon," he said. "help me gather up these leaves and lay them in a pile, and then you can start to work."

"Tomorrow's Mommie's birthday," Johnny said.

"It is? You sure of that?"

"Ginnie Lee says so. Says she's baking a orange-frosting cake. So I'm going to make a bracelet and a necklace for Mommie."

"Well, that's a good idea," his father answered.

"Where you going, Daddy?"

"Just off a minute," he said. "Just down here a ways."

"You going away, Daddy?"

"Just down here to help someone," his father said. "Someone's lost the way."

"Will you come right back?"

"I'll be right back, son. You make Mommie a birthday present."

"A lady's lost the way," Johnny talked to himself, "I can smell a lady."

He wove the leaves into a long necklace, tying the ends together, and then more into a bracelet, and he could feel afternoon going. It was a long time before Daddy came back and when he did, he was whistling.

"You happy?" he called out. "Daddy, you happy?"

"I guess I am, big fellow," his father said. "I guess I am, all right."

"It isn't afternoon any more."

"It still is," Jack said, "It's just very late in the afternoon."

Afternoon near five-thirty and the stranger ripped the Scotch tape from the letter, sitting in the cell in the courthouse near the Wheel.

20.

D_{EAR} *Maur,*
> *This, over a nightcap. . .*

I've been thinking, all the way down here—oh, and long before that, when we first spoke of divorce, and all through the divorce, and during the dismal aftermath, that it all started when we got mixed up with the couch clique. Remember? I can remember so damn clearly the night we had drinks with Julie at The Drake, and he said: "No kidding, analysis made a new man of me," and I saw that little light bulb go on in your head, and you said: "How do you go about it?"

Julie said, "What do you mean?"

You said, "I mean, how do you start it? Do you just walk in and say, 'Look, I'm all screwed up?' and I knew that's exactly what'd you be just walking in and saying the next afternoon to some psychiatrist.

*Because we **were** having terrible fights then, weren't we, Maur? I remember it because every place we went that* *song from* High Noon *was playing (Do not desert me, O my darling) and we were always in the midst of an argument when it would come singing over the radio in our bedroom, or come pumped into some cocktail lounge when we were raging at each other. And if we were on a street corner, someone would come by humming it, and it seemed to haunt the days and nights. We'd been to see* The Shrike *the night we met Julie, and I remember what you said during inermission:*

"I brought the original with me," and a week later there was an intruder in our house, an uninvited guest who stayed with us until we split up, ate meals with us, fought with us, made up with us, went out with us, made up our party lists with us, even tried making love with us— we fooled him there, though—and sent us a bill for $420 a month. How well I remember the figure, every month on the check stub, and the name: Dr. Feldman.

It was Dr. Feldman would say this and Dr. Feldman would say that, and Dr. Feldman thinks this, and Dr. Feldman thinks that, and before very long we had another guest to keep Dr. Feldman busy, and her name was Dr. Mannerheim. She was my check stub.

Then we didn't even bother arguing with each other any more. We just mixed our nightcaps and let Dr. Feldman and Dr. Mannerheim argue, like proper mediums, never interfering with the messages, but rolling them out rote-style, until pretty soon it had nothing to do with Maur and Deel, but with what was left of Maur and Deel. The neuroses.

I was a neurosis who married a father-image because I feared sex, translated from the Freud as incest, and you were a neurosis who satisfied me because you were impotent and I had nothing to fear from you because you too feared sex, translated from the Freud as incest.

We wiggled and squirmed under the microscopes as pretty as any two neuroses could for the doctors, and in our new-found microcosm we collected dreams and slips of speech and prescriptions for tranquilizers, and we told time by the fifty-minute hour.

None of it seems real now, Maur, nor fair, nor honest— just glib and pat and too much like tennis. Anyone can play.

I always hated taking the scalpel to emotions, and I

still don't like it—but you accused me, right before our split, of still holding back. And you were right. So if we can save anything, if all the sawdust hasn't spilled out by now, let's patch it with facts.

I told you at Missouri about the abortion, told you then about this thing I had for types like Duboe and how I made Jud feel responsible. I told you too that I couldn't marry Chad because I was afraid of that side of me. I knew how strong it was. But you said I couldn't go through with my marriage with Chad because I didn't love him— that much was true—I never loved anyone but you—and you said I didn't love him because I didn't want any kind of relationship but the kind we had. You wanted to believe that. I did too—even that, instead of the truth that Dr. Mannerheim dug out with her pad and pencil.

But there were things in the way: a cab driver one night—the night you were sick after we came back from our honeymoon, and I'd gone down to London Terrace for dinner at Dru's. A TV repairman, one afternoon, six months later. In Juan les Pins, the beach bum who paraded as the squash player, and in Florence, Emilio—the guide from the Pitti Palace. There was a deck steward on the Liberté, and a fellow I met down in the Village when I was buying you a pair of space shoes. Others, too.

And Maur, every time I hated myself afterward, but it didn't stop me.

For a while Mannerheim had me thinking I was a Lesbian and you were a fairy—and then I began to think Mannerheim was a Lesbian and Feldman was a fairy— and all the while this was going on, you were saying we were getting better.

Our nightcaps went from four to six a night that spring, and in June for an anniversary present, you gave me a gold pillbox from Cartier—for my Miltown.

You said we were getting better.

I don't remember when it was we got well enough, in your opinion, to start talking about divorce. Maybe you do. Because I never felt well enough for that, if that's what it took.

When you called me in Las Vegas and asked me to come back, when you said—remember, Maur?—"I guess we're both pretty peculiar people, Deel, but I know something. I love you!" I was too battle-scarred, or too proud, or maybe just too goddam tranquilized to do anything but hang up on you—and after it was over, I was dazed.

Now I'm back home, or back in Bastrop—because home isn't here, there's nothing here but unpleasantness to remember, except for the day you came here and took me away—and Maur, that seemed as much a miracle then as our getting together again seems now—but you came. I would have married Chad, I suppose, and gone on living the image other people saw, and he saw—and probably one day I would have gotten into trouble, real small-town trouble, like the last time when he was at war, but you got the vibrations, didn't you? Remember how we used to believe we had E.S.P. or folie à deux; or that we were enchanted—our own magic?

Now it's gone. But Maur, I haven't been taking those don't-give-a-damn pills any more, and I find I do give a damn. If we needed pills at all, maybe we needed do-give-a-damn ones. Because we lost something, Maur. Maybe it wasn't much, but it was all I ever had, or wanted—you. And you!

Deel.

21.

TWILIGHT

and he pulled himself to his feet, holding his jaw where he'd been punched, leaning against the fence, breathless, with his stomach still aching, sometime after six; still light out.

He heard the pickup go down the street at a wild pace and remembered the angry words: "You dare show up looking that way, do you?"

Gradually he could straighten his body and walk, gradually, inching steps, up the gravel path to his house.

He found Cass in the kitchen. Johnny-Bob was in the bathroom in the hallway. He could hear the water running. The child hadn't heard it; he had run ahead.

"Cass, I—"

She looked up at him. She was running water, holding her hand under the faucet at the sink, waiting for it to warm up.

"People have been calling you all afternoon," she said. "Your army!"

He leaned against the table, watching her. The water was steaming and she pulled her hand back quickly, then reached for the sink's plug. "Johnny-Bob is filthy! Looks as if he's been rolling in mud! Weren't you watching him?"

"What was your father doing here?" he said in a dull tone; his stomach still hurt from the first punch and his jaw was swelling. "Or didn't you know he was waiting out front for me?"

"He was waiting all afternoon for you," she said, with her back turned to him. "He was only *one* of your visitors."

"I know about Dee," he said.

She stopped what she was doing, but didn't look at him. Cass had a great facility for imitating someone's voice in such perfect mock style that it was hard to suppress laughter, and she was imitating Dee's now, with all the breathless, husky qualities, standing with the dish towel around her waist: "How nice to see you, Cassandra! I really can't stay. I came to see Chad on business, something of a personal nature. I hope you'll understand, Cassandra!"

She said in her own voice, syrupy-sweet: "Why, Delia, dear old bean-girl, how love-ah-ly to see you once again! Why, of course I understand, ducks. You'll find I am one of the most understanding women in the whole of Tate County, Delia, lamb! Now, you'll find my sweet, handsome, virile and irresistible husband is out at the Dip with our child, but don't let that bother you, dear, ducky Dee-Benny, because our child can't see anything—" her voice broke—"anyway."

He went across to her, and it was just as she broke away from his hands that she seemed to explode.

"I've had it, Chad! Up to here! I've had it—do you hear me!"

She did a ridiculous thing then. She began to push sudsy water at him from the sink in front of her, spraying it on his clothes with her hands, like a child in a water-fight.

From behind them Johnny-Bob said: "Who's splashing?"

"Mommie's splashing!" she shouted, giving the water another wallop with her hand. Then, wild-eyed, she turned and ran from the room, the dish towel trailing in the wet on the floor. He heard her noise on the stairs.

"Is Mommie playing?" Johnny-Bob asked.

"That's right, honey. Mommie's playing." Chad wiped the floor with the towel.

"She was going to wash me," he said. "I'm all dirty."

"C'mere, big fellow, Daddy'll wash you," Chad answered.

He guided his son to the kitchen sink, and he reached for his rag and the soap, he saw his face in the mirror—there where his jaw was swelling, was the smudge of lipstick.

Upstairs the bathroom door slammed shut.

"Look," Poppy Porter said at *twilight,* "I know he's not there yet, but when he comes there I wish you'd tell him to call me."

Arnold Belden stood behind her. "Calm down," he said. "It's hard to hear long-distance if you shout, Poppy."

She muffled the receiver with her hand. "He's so stupid! I know just who he is—the big fat one that chews the cigar all the time!"

She said into the receiver: "When he gets there, will you have him call me, Mr. Hodges? . . . Well, of course he's coming there. Didn't you call him and tell him to? He left late this afternoon for Montgomery? . . . You don't?"

Arnold Belden walked over and sat down, picked up a magazine; then threw it aside. He saw Poppy drop the arm of the telephone back into its cradle.

"Well," she said, "well, Daddy, he never called Troy."

"You sure Troy said it was Hodges?"

"He said he had to go to Montgomery on business. That's who he always stays with—Hodges or that other fat slob!"

"Easy, honey!"

"Well, they are fat slobs, Daddy! And if Troy really had any business to go to so suddenly they'd know about it! But they don't. They said Troy wasn't coming back for another week, as far as they knew!"

"Then where is he?"

"Where do you think he is?" Poppy said. "He's in hiding someplace. The big old politician, afraid he'll get his picture in the paper with the Negroes! He's run out, Daddy! Till the heat's off! His home and his family and everydab-body be damned, but his praise-be-to-Allah constituents!"

"I don't want to believe that of Troy," Arnold Belden said.

"Do you think I do?" Poppy was screaming now, at *twilight's end.*

Beneath the tall elms, in the black background of the big tree trunks, with the moon rising, and a bugle sounding the minor four-note call, going two by two like an army of coupled ghosts, the formless flopping sheets moving solemnly in the still night air, at Chandler's; white robes with pants-legs ends and shoes, yellow pairs with knobby toes, high-tops laced with mud-encrusted ties; shoes that knew the fields and the hills; circling to form an arc near the platform of the gin.

And there the cross burning; the air heavy with the stink of kerosene; and then the sound:

"He said it was sick! For niggers to crawl like venom through the corridors of our school! And they took him to jail for it! He said it was sick! For black niggers to watch white legs and lust after white daughters of white fathers and- mothers! And they took him to jail for it! He said it was sick! He said it was sick!"

And the roar: "And it is!"

And the roar: "And it is!"

And the roar: "Sick!"

And the chant: "Sick! Sick! Sick! Sick" of the black silhouettes against the white cloth in the orange light of the flame at *night* for the stranger knew a Spam sandwich and a cell, and the jailer playing Elvis Presley records off in the back room by himself: " *. . . you're nothing but a hound dog and you ain't no good to me.*" and *night* knew a plan to have a dream—a woman like her—like she was, Dee—so beautiful in church, kneeling, never mind, he sank his hands into his pockets, now he *could.* And she was his right, her kind—a woman like that, a rich, soft expensive woman—his! His heritage!

When he used to come home on vacation—remember—from the military school in the blue uniform with the gold braid and the visor cap, God! Anyone of them out in Pelham, and all of them out in Pelham—eying him, in the blue uniform with the gold braid, touching the gold buttons with their fingers.

He knew what her guts were about, and he could have her. He wasn't afraid now; she was no better than he was. If she didn't believe him, he had the letter. He could read it out loud in The Wheel, but he wouldn't. He'd say he would.

She'd said to the man out front of church: "Arrest him? Are you crazy?"

Then she *did* like him; even in church she'd grinned at him. Hadn't she? When he followed her in?

Always he'd stood on the fringes of what was rightly his, of what he was born into, and Lennie Gold used to laugh: "Ahhh, forget it, Richard! You're so rotten drunk. So you had money once! So you could have had any woman you wanted—even Lana Turner! My heart bleeds, for Christ's sake! And everyone knew who you were back in smelly Pelham! Your story touches my heart, boy!" But Lennie never knew the pain-haunted memories. The way he'd defiled himself—his birthright, trying to recapture its essence.

Now the night knew a plan to have a dream—a woman like her—and laurel! He'd be gentle with her too. Now he wasn't afraid any more.

Standing there in the cell, suddenly he realized the music had stopped. Footsteps came down the corridor.

"You sure kicked up a riot," the jailer groaned, itching himself around the waist where his shirt was pulled out, exposing his white belly. "The Ku is out marching. Ku ain't marched around here in some time. You sure did it!"

"There's reporters down from Birmingham, *I* hear," Richard Buddy said. "Don't you have anything better than canned meat?"

"We ain't had nothing but niggers in this jail overnight for six months," the jailer yawned. "Niggers think it's turkey . . . Yeah, there's reporters being put up down to the hotel. You sure kicked up a riot. And let me tell you something else: you gonna be searched."

"Searched? I *was*."

"Naw, this time for personal property belonging to Miss Delia Benjamin. Chief's coming down here. You sure kicked up a riot to get him outa his fat nest on Sunday night, fellow."

"When's he coming?"

"Phoned up just now," the jailer said. "And something else too."

"What's that?"

"I ain't no nigger-lover myself. Goddam niggers come in here and smell up the place and I gotta wait on 'em. I ain't no nigger-lover. I'd ride with the Ku any time—" he gave a snort—"if they was ridin'. Go around in cars these days—but that's ridin' I guess—"

Buddy interrupted him. "What's the something else?"

"It's downstairs," the jailer said. "I can't let him up 'cause it's against the law. But I can take anything down to him you might want him to keep for you. Duboe's down there. Come in with the Ku. They're heading for the Nelly."

"Okay," Richard Buddy said, "but I need a plain envelope, see? And I want you to listen to instructions."

"You'd think you was the jailer and I was where you is," the fellow answered, "but I guess you know your business. Them niggers think Spam is turkey," he said, shuffling away back down the corridor. "Gobble it up jest like turkey with their big mouths."

Richard Buddy looked through bars smiling at night.

Night. Out in his yard he said to her, "But the important thing is I *know* now, Cass. She doesn't mean one damn thing any more. I can say that honestly. Will you come on back in the house? You can't stay out here all night."

"How do I know you're not lying? You must have lied all these years when you said you loved me. You *must* have!"

She sat in the canvas-back campchair, her back to him, swatting the mosquitoes as they ate her arms and legs.

He remembered another night they had stood the war of mosquitoes out in Senior Porter's backyard, after Troy shoved Poppy into the antique glass collection of his mother's; that time Poppy had said in drunken anger for everyone to hear: "You're a Beggsom poor-white, and no war-profit education down at Alabam can clean the smell off you, Cassie! You don't belong! You look like a Polish maid on Sunday with your hair all frizzed up—look at you!"

And the mosquitoes had fed on their flesh while she cried: "Poppy's right, Chad! I'm all wrong! My perm is frizzy and I don't know how to dress—*never* did—even the Pi Phi's couldn't teach me how to keep from being tacky, and you just feel sorry for me. Everyone says it—not just Poppy!"

"I want to marry you," he had told her for the first time. "I want to get us out of this mosquito-night and take you with me, and I'll never leave you, Cass. Never!"

"Cassie," he said, "Cass—listen. Whatever's happened, and the good Lord knows you and me have been through some big hell together, I love you. I came out in the mosquitoes once before to tell you that, remember? Well, here we are back and I've got the same thing to say."

He could hear her crying now, but he didn't go to her yet. She was still in a state. He saw her hand grip the hankie.

He said a sixth time, must have been: "Dee wanted me to get that letter from that fellow they locked up. That's all she wanted. And Cass, while we were standing there talking, while I was watching our kid make those leaves into a birthday necklace for you, I suddenly knew I never loved anyone like you—like I love you, Cass. I suddenly knew that. And I felt like telling Dee that I didn't have any hard feelings about what happened years back—because I meant it. I felt like hearing myself say it because I knew right there it was true. And Cass, she said she was glad—that's all, and she meant she was. That's when I got the lipstick on my chin. She said she was glad that things worked out so neither of us regretted what happened, and she kissed my chin. I don't love Dee, Cass. I love you. Hear?"

"How come she isn't Benny any more," she said.

He could tell by her voice she was smiling.

He said, "She just isn't. Now, will you come in and stop feeding us to the mus'keets!"

"I've got to tell you something else," she said, turning toward him now, half-sitting on the edge of the campchair, as though she would not budge until everything was settled between them. "Papa says he knows the man behind what's happening tomorrow. He says you're going to get in trouble if you escort the Nigra children to school, but he says nothing's going to happen to Johnny-Bob."

"Did you think something was?"

"We got a threatening note this afternoon mentioning Johnny-Bob. It said our child wouldn't be safe if you escorted the Nigras to school. Papa took it with him. He wanted to find out who wrote it."

"I'll bet he did!"

"Chad—"

"Okay," he said. "But have we got to fight that now?"

"Poppy got one too, threatening the twins. She called me right before you came home. Troy had to go to Montgomery and she was upset, wanted to talk to you."

"I'll call her. Then Troy's out, hmm? It's just me and Jud—because honey, I've got to do that!"

"I wanted to tell you," she said, "that I don't feel the way I did about it. If you think you have to, well, then—"

"Thanks, Cass."

"But Chad—" she stood up now; still by the chair. She said, "Papa isn't a part of this, Chad. I know he isn't. I want you to know it. I want you to tell me you know it."

Jack Chadwick swallowed hard.

"All right," he said, "all right. Maybe for once old John's keeping his nose clean. But he sure packed me a wallop!"

"He must have seen the lipstick," she said, coming toward him in the night.

Night, at the Nelly, with Turner Towers saying, "Naw, no! I won't go out there and say anything like that!"

"They're coming," Tappie said. "They're two houses down de road. You gotta, Turner."

The deacon said, "Your grandmaw's right, son. We're not Birmingham-big; we're little here in the Nelly. We got to eat crow for this mob, son! Tomorrow maybe, when they're back in the hills, we can hold our heads up—"

"Maybe, Deacon! Maybe! Our kids are going to school here tomorrow!" He slammed his fist into his palm. "Do you think they aren't?"

"Tonight's tonight. Tomorrow's tomorrow. This is a Ku Klux outside, boy! You have a family to think about now!"

Doris Towers got up and went across the room to her husband, touched his sleeve. "Turner, I'd tell you if you were right, if I thought you were, and you know that. But we're just little in number, Turner. Big hope and big in prayer, but awful little in number."

"I'm tired of being little and black! God damn it, are we just helpless?"

"Let dem answer for you," Tappie said, "Dey coming. Marching wid that cross down de night."

Night, with the grotesque black holes for eyes in the sheets and the chant: "Sick! Sick! Sick! Sick!"

"Here, stop here!" against the moonlight soft drooping willow branches, by the shack at the end of the block.

"C'mon out!" was shouted.

And the tension in the minute's wait, while the door opened on the crack of light, and the dark figure walked slowly toward them, slump-shouldered, head down.

"Name, boy?"

"Towers." Hot breaths waiting for the "sir" at the end.

"What are you?"

"A nigger." Sigh-pause. "Sir!" Tired.

"What are you always going to be?"

"A good nigger, sir." Resigned.

"And a good nigger don't go to school with whites, does he, because that's sick. Isn't it, boy?"

"Yes, sir, it's sick."

"Yes, siree, boy, it is sick!"

While the cross went back to the shoulders, and the ghosts went on parade; and the chant: "Sick!" and the figure standing before the shack, bent like someone old, and "Sick! Sick! Sick! Sick!" shouted down the night.

22.

MONDAY MORNING

the pickets appeared outside the Bastrop High School.

"Just hang on tight," Jud said, coming up Love Lucy Hill, two children with him, one on either side, holding his hands, "and don't look to left or right."

A crowd formed along the walks of the school—the curious, the angry, the excited.

"And don't pay any attention to anyone," Jack Chadwick said to the pair he walked with. "It's okay." They came out of the Nelly.

Down at the courthouse, the judge was sifting through the evidence against Richard Buddy, and deciding there wasn't any. His daughter was staying at home until the niggers got the notion of going to school alongside her out of their heads. ·

"What's your favorite subject?" Poppy Porter asked the trio walking with her. "I always liked English best." Passing over the brim of the hill, facing the long walk that led ahead.

Someone shouted: "Here come the niggers!"

And the chanting was drowned out by the wail of a hundred sirens, coming in from State I, passing the cotton that whitewashed the fields where black faces paused in picking to stare, weaving past the rows of furs and cedars, golden poplars and the elms and Judas trees, up West Tennessee and down Court to another shout:

"Troopers!"

And again: "Niggers! Sick Niggers!"

"Keep ahold," Jud said.

Chad said, "Steady, now. It's okay."

And Poppy Porter looked at the man who jumped out of the car behind the troopers and said: "Troy!"

"Go on home, now," he told her. "I think we can control things now!"

Then it was eight-fifteen, and by eight-thirty tear gas was holding back the more stubborn element in the mob outside Bastrop High, and inside, Asa Towers, cousin to Turner, was turning to "The fourth page of the Composition Book," the teacher said. "We'll leave the opening pages to record quiz marks. We'll write our first composition on a simple subject. What it means to live in America."

Heads bowed to the task.

Beside Asa a towheaded teen-ager began to scribble: "It means going to school with jig-a-boos," writing, smirking.

And behind Asa, a brown-haired boy wrote: "It means what happened here in Bastrop, Alabama, today. I mean —" frowning, biting his pencil, and then rubbing out *I mean,* he wrote—"In front of me there's a Negro boy about my own age sitting at his desk. It means that . . ."

At eight-thirty:

"I'm hungry," Jud said at the corner to the other two. "I'm going back and fix me some breakfast."

Troy waved as he went: "I suppose," he said to Chadwick, "there'll be all sorts of reports about the thug in the crowd who broke the reporter's camera."

"I don't know about that," Chad answered him, "but I'll be damned if I don't think I'm going to vote a straight ticket this year, Senator."

"Not yet," Troy laughed, "not by a damn sight. Do you think we can hold the fort, Chad?"

"I think so."

"If not, there's six hundred National Guard and twelve tanks where those boys came from."

Across the street a horn honked.

"Looks like Dee," Troy said. He poked Chad in the ribs. "She still chasing you?"

And down at the Wheel the stranger was setting up a box to stand on, that Monday morning that found Mrs. Benjamin cowering in the Chandler kitchen, before Duboe, who was grinning, holding his sides, his knubby fingers slipped into the loops of his jeans:

"You heard what I said," he said. "A friend of mine entrusted this little old letter to me. A-yeah! In fact, I wasn't even supposed to read its contents, ma'am, but you know I'm a curious one. Want me to read it again?"

"No!"

"Then if you want it back to protect your daughter's good name," Duboe giggled, "you gonna do what I say, hear? A-yeah! You gonna do as I say, Mrs. Benjamin, if you want this here letter! Now, how about it?"

And the muse Terpsichore was no longer voluble, on Monday morning, near noon, John Beggsom saw Jack Chadwick and Delia Benjamin park outside his place.

Crabb Suggs was standing with him in the back, and old John saw them from the window.

"He's got a nerve!" Beggsom said. "Lookit them sitting out there in broad daylight!"

"There's not time now," Suggs said. "Worry that some other time. Buddy's got to have a place to come to. They got troopers all over the place, but you got that shack."

"I can't put him up," Beggsom said, still watching out the window at the car parked there in the sun. "It's too dangerous."

"Just overnight. They be looking for us both. I'll stay out to my sister's in Morrow."

"Lookit them, goddam them!"

"C'mon, John, I gotta have an answer fast. It's twenty to twelve now, and school breaks at noon."

"I don't want no trouble, though," Beggsom said.

Near noon they could laugh about it, and they were laughing now.

"But I was scared, Chad," she said. "I'd started off to see what was going on down at the school, and I'd gone back for my cigarettes when I saw Mother with them. The look on her face, Chad, gaw, I—" and she began to laugh again, her shoulders shaking. "But I was really scared."

"Well," he said, "we got the letter back."

"And Mrs. Chandler is now a member of the Methodist muses, asked in person by Terpsichore. Gaw, Chad."

"I hope you get rid of that thing." He glanced down at the wadded up paper in her lap. "Was it all that bad?"

She looked away, beginning to tear it as she talked. "Poor Mama. She wouldn't even look at me afterward."

Jack Chadwick said, "Aw, I think she was just mad because Mrs. Gus spat at her."

"Poor, poor Mama," Dee repeated, sighing. "I was always her trial, I guess."

Jack Chadwick pushed down the door handle. "I want to call Cass," he said. "Could you stand a Coke?"

She said, "Sure could."

Beggsom was still watching them from the window.

He turned abruptly and yelled to the Negro out front: "I ain't here, see?"

Then he went through the back door, out and around to the side of his place, springing the blade in his jacknife, scowling.

At noon "Everything's fine," Cass said, "I just talked to Jud over the telephone when Chad called. He said Arnold was having lunch brought into the school. There are still some picketers, but for the most part things have quieted down."

She said, "I'm proud of you, Jack. Can you hear me?"

And the whistles blew in twelve o'clock with a crash

that sent a rock flying through Turner Tower's store window down by the tracks, while the Negro boy out at Beggsom's Place slid into the telephone booth after Chad, and Chad said to Dee at the table: "We might as well have a bite to eat right here. What do you say? It's lunchtime."

23.

MONDAY AFTERNOON

at one o'clock when they were finishing their sandwiches at Beggsom's place it happened.

"What happened?" Jack Chadwick asked, looking up suddenly at the trooper in the doorway, but the trooper brushed past him, went on out through the back of Beggsom's place.

"He said he was searching." Dee dropped a crust on the paper plate and wadded up her napkin.

"Yes, but searching for *what?*"

"I don't know," she said, "but here comes Cass." They both looked out the open door to see Cass Chadwick running up from the car. "In Mama's car, of all things!" Dee said.

Cass Chadwick was breathless. "I almost didn't make it. I kept watching the meter sink down to empty."

"What is it?" Jack said. "What's happened?"

"Jud was beaten up—when he was coming from his house after lunch. I got a frantic call from your mother, Dee. She was near to hysterics and I ran over there. When I tried to call from there this line was busy. I tried and tried, and then I just got in her car and came on out here? They've got Jud at Benjamin's still—he's pretty bad off. I heard the troopers were heading out here and I just got scared for you, Chad, and for Papa. Is Papa all right?"

"I haven't even seen him," Chad said.

A trooper came in from the rear. "Who called to say they were going to hide out here?" he wanted to know. "A colored boy, sounded like. Said he knew there'd be trouble and the guilty parties would head out here. Where's he at?"

"He was here a minute ago," Jack said, "but we didn't know anything about it."

"Well, he called up down to the police station," the trooper stood there aimlessly.

"You better go to your place, Dee," Cass said. "Your mother's in a state! Jud'll need you too. The doctor's with him, but he's hurt bad, Dee!" and as Dee started, Cass said, "Wait, don't take the car until there's more gas in it. The meter's way down. There's a pump outside."

"Take my car," Chad said. "The keys are in it."

The trooper asked, "Whose car's that out behind. Says Suggs Store on the side."

"That's who beat up Jud," Cass cried. "Suggs and that stranger!"

"Then they did come this way." The trooper scratched under his cap. "Where in hell are they, then?"

Dee swung onto State I and pushed her foot hard on the pedal. She was not thinking of her mother now, but of Jud, and of the worst that could happen to him, but not without his knowing, no God, she prayed, not without his knowing the truth. If she ever wanted to tell the truth in her life it was now, and she drove to get faster to the time when she could, thinking why couldn't I have had the guts to do it yesterday, when I knew in the vestry what he was remembering, or last night, when he walked across the street and sat with me on the front porch, and said in that flat, solemn pronouncement: "I still love you, Dee. I still never forgive myself."

She drove so fast the car swayed with the curves, but she was a good driver and she knew the winds and twists of this road better than any other, knew when it broke to gravel down near the Dip and didn't slow for the dust it always kicked up in that spot, and she was rounding the bend for the twin hills near town when she became aware she had a rider:

"You want to kill us, Deel," he said.

She heard the name "Deel" with a certain leap to her heart, and then she saw his face. Her rider was the stranger, Richard Buddy.

"I want you to head off down here where we can turn around. I want you to go to Chandlers'," he said.

"I'm going to town," she told him. "I don't care where you're going."

"I got your letter," he said, "in safe keeping. You better turn around or I'm going to read your letter down at the Wheel before the whole crowd, Deel."

She laughed, knowing the lie, remembering how she had ripped that letter to shreds. "You just do that!"

"I mean it!" he said. He began to climb over to the front seat, his legs first, then his arms, one on her shoulder, one on the steering wheel. "We're going to ride a crooked mile, Deel, until you head back. And you're going to, you know. Now do as I say, head back!"

He moved a foot over near the brake pedal.

"Are you crazy, on *this* road?" she said. "Do you want to wreck the car!"

"I want to turn around," he said, "and I'm going to see that we do."

He touched his foot to hers, then pressed hard.

She could feel the sting when he clamped his shoe against the skin of her ankle, and then she heard the sound like a gun. The car's wheel flew from her grasp like a berserk spring.

24.

THE END

of the school day, came at the top of Love Lucy Hill where Asa Turner turned to the tall brown-haired boy who had walked with him. Said: "Thanks, Alan."

There were others milling around, a few picketers who had followed them, the six white boys and the seven Negro children, and a reporter and a photographer.

"Shake hands, boys," the photographer said.

The brown-haired boy turned: "We don't have to. I don't shake hands normally."

A flash-bulb went off and the six Negroes started on down the hill, but Asa lingered.

"I can go on my own steam tomorrow," he said to the brown-haired boy.

"You want to repeat what you just said, colored boy?" the reporter asked. He smiled at Asa. "It's all right. I want it for the folks to read. This is real democracy."

"You don't give us a chance," the brown-haired boy said. "You're worse then those with the signs." He waved at Asa. "See you tomorrow," he said. Another flash of light beamed from the camera. "Here," the brown-haired boy pointed to where he stood. "I'll pick you up around eight-ten."

Asa said, "You don't have to."

"I know I don't," the boy said. "See you." He waved again.

Behind Asa a big man carrying a picket sign yelled: "Sick!"

"Stand over here," the reporter said, "so I can get you both in. Glare at him, Rastus, just like you was doin'."

The big man moved to get into the shot, but Asa ran down the hill, grinning.

"Sick!" the big man shouted from the top of Love Lucy, his eye on the camera. But the camera pointed away and down; and the guard came over the lens.

"That's all for now," the photographer said. "We'll get more in town tonight when your boy speaks at the Wheel, but right now that's it." The big man hesitated. "That's all for now," the photographer repeated.

The reporter sighed: "Guess we might as well head out to the highway and see what that crash was all about."

"I'm pooped," the photographer said, "I'm going back to the hotel and nap."

Out on the highway the troopers gathered around the car, smashed and swinging on a crane, the fields still clinging to it.

"Yep, wheels were slashed all right," one said, "both the front ones. But it was the front left that did it. Blew out. Other one held up."

"Both might have," a second said, "but she was doing some fancy twisting with them, looks like from the burn marks."

"Where are the bodies beautiful?" another said.

"There was only one of that caliber. She's at the hospital. Other one's on a slab, I suppose, waiting to go to grass."

"Yep, wheels were slashed all right," the first one yawned. "Haul her off!" he yelled at the driver of the pickup. "Geee-hoah!" He wiped his face in the hot afternoon sun.

"Hound Dog" was playing in the background down at the jail.

Cass Chadwick came down the long corridor leading away from the cells and out into the bare-walled waiting room where Chad stood waiting.

"Yes," she said. "That's the answer."

"But why?"

"Beggsom blood," she said. "Same reason I can't hate him for it. He almost killed you, but when I saw him in there crying, I couldn't hate him anymore, Chad. He said he did it because he thought you and Dee were doing more behind my back. Said after he did it he came to our house to be with me, and when I was gone and he heard I'd gone out to you, he said he had to call and warn me not to get in your car. He couldn't get the line. The colored boy left the phone off the hook after he warned the troopers, afraid they'd call back and check and he'd get in trouble. So Papa called the police."

"Too late."

She looked up at his face when she heard the tone of his voice.

"Too late," he repeated. Then he said, "Dee died an hour ago."

By dinner time that night, Jud was well enough to sit up. Poppy and Troy had him at their house, and Troy was the one who told him.

Jud said, "Did her mother tell her about the wire?"

"She never came to after the crash," Troy answered. "What about the wire?"

"It was sent to the house this afternoon when I was resting up over there. Mrs. Benjamin was so excited the whole time she ripped it open without seeing who it was for. It was from New York. Peculiar. Just one word."

He sighed, rubbing his eyes with his hand tiredly, "Just said *vibrations.*"

"Whatever that means," Troy Porter shrugged his shoulders helplessly.

The end of that time came at evening down at the Wheel.

For a while there had been the chants of "sick-sick-sick," strong at first, then petering out in a sigh, while a small crowd milled around the box on the green lawn, under the ginkgo tree. Across the street, the reporter sat on the curb, doodling aimlessly on his note pad; and behind him, the photographer, rested from his nap, lolled around the flagpole, pulling threads from his coat and filing down his nails.

The big man was in the crowd still carrying the same picket sign he had carried to Love Lucy hill, and now and then he spoke out about the "niggers" and "the sick Supreme Court." But at one point a voice shouted: "How's Jud Forsythe? Who knows *that?*"

And some looked at the big man, threatening him with their eyes; and the big man was silent.

"I guess the jails are full up tonight," someone cackled. "And the morgue," another, deep-sounding, desultory. They shuffled around uninspired, looking awkward and lost and pointless.

"No one's coming," a thin little man spoke out. "No one left to come."

"We're here, though," a voice said weakly.

Then a new voice spoke up, a loud, strong voice: "We ought to all go on home," it said. "Who was he anyway? Some Yankee! Some butting-in Northerner! What'd he know about Jud Forsythe? What'd he know about any of us? Where'd he come from?"

"Ask me," the thin little man said, "*he* was sick!"

"We ought to all go on home," the new voice said. "Who was he to chase-ass himself down here and run our affairs for us? We run our own goddam affairs!"

"We ought to all go on home," the big man said, dropping his picket sign. "Who was he?"

Across the street the reporter pulled himself to his feet. "They're breaking up, looks like," he said. "Crowd's thinning out."

"They'll be out again tomorrow," the photographer said.

"Naw, I don't think so," his colleague answered. "There was a turning point somewhere during the middle of the day, along about noon, when that preacher fellow got the beating."

"You just don't pound on a man of the cloth," the photographer said.

Together they walked down Court in the hot evening.

THE END
of a Gold Medal Original by
VIN PACKER

www.ingramcontent.com/pod-product-compliance
Lightning Source LLC
Chambersburg PA
CBHW010641100726
47900CB00011B/2916